TO KISS A KING

NICOLE BURNHAM

Royal
Scandals
San Rimini

To Kiss a King

by Nicole Burnham

Cover design by Patricia Schmitt

Edition: July 2020
ISBN: 9978-1-941828-53-3 (paperback)
ISBN: 978-1-941828-52-6 (ebook)
ISBN: 978-1-941828-54-0 (audio)

For more information or to subscribe to Nicole's newsletter, visit nicoleburnham.com.

CHAPTER 1

"GOOD MORNING, Your Highness. How was your time with Greta this morning?"

King Eduardo diTalora cast a sidelong glance at his longtime personal assistant, Luisa Borelli, as she fell into step beside him. Polished as always, she wore a soft brown skirt and tailored jacket with low heels. Her black hair was twisted into a flawless knot at her nape and tiny gold studs dotted her earlobes.

Luisa was very good at her job. One would never know by looking at her that she was also the devil incarnate.

Eduardo shook his head, then looked forward, his smile encompassing various staff members who lingered in the hallway, waiting for him to arrive at his office. To Luisa, he said, "It wouldn't be a proper Monday morning if Greta hadn't spent the weekend plotting new ways to torture me."

"Precisely which part of the session did you find torturous, Your Highness? The box jumps?"

"No, because she decided to change the box jump portion of the workout to stepping onto the box—"

"Oh, good—"

"While holding a fifteen-kilo medicine ball."

"Oh."

"Then she added a series of planks. Apparently, running is insufficient for building core strength. I attempted to convince her otherwise, but she refused to listen to my wisdom."

"She is stubborn that way. But I daresay that when it comes to matters of health and fitness, Greta is usually right."

"As is the cousin who referred her and wouldn't stop nagging me until I hired her." He raised a brow at Luisa, but buffered it with a smile that she returned.

Eduardo wished one of the guards a good morning as he and Luisa rounded the final corner to his office, then Luisa said, "It's my duty to ensure you serve the country to the best of your ability. Maintaining a high level of fitness is essential to that task. If it makes you feel better, tomorrow I've scheduled a run at six a.m. The weather should be ideal. Mild and clear with low wind."

Most people would consider a sunrise run torture, but to Eduardo, a crack of dawn jaunt along San Rimini's waterfront or through the hills above the palace sounded like heaven. He could breathe fresh air, listen to music, and allow his mind to wander. For that single hour, he was responsible to no one but himself, and there was no Greta at his side to insist he could work harder or crank out one more rep.

If he could crank out one more rep, he was the type to do so without being told.

Eduardo greeted a courier who waited near Luisa's desk, then glanced at his assistant. "I'd be obliged if there are waffles in the dining room following that run tomorrow. Samuel had oatmeal today. Good oatmeal, but still oatmeal."

"I'll see what I can do, though Samuel mentioned that he's planning on baked quinoa with berries."

"I'll pretend I didn't hear that."

"Perhaps you could pretend it's a waffle?"

"I shall pretend I didn't hear that, either. I'll pretend you said, 'Yes, Your Highness, I will request waffles and ensure Samuel provides plenty of syrup. Perhaps a few of those berries on the side.'"

Luisa raised a finger to indicate that the courier should wait for her, then she and Eduardo entered his formal office. Eduardo's chief political advisor, Sergio Ribisi, sat on a sofa beside Eduardo's press secretary, a burly young man named Zeno Amendola who looked better suited to commanding a rugby team than a press room. The two were hunched over a tablet, reviewing what Eduardo assumed were notes for their morning meeting. Across from them sat Margaret Halaby, his Director of Charities and Patronages. Margaret had her hands in her lap, a pen threaded between her fingers. A notepad lay on the sofa beside her, its top page filled with indiscernible scribbles, bullet points, and arrows. She stared past the two men, lost in thought.

Luisa made a small noise to catch their attention. All three rose in unison and wished Eduardo a good morning. He waved them back into their seats, then asked Luisa to give him a five-minute warning before he needed to leave for his first event of the day.

"How was your session with Greta?" Zeno asked once Luisa closed the door behind her.

He nailed Zeno with a glare. The man had the audacity to grin in return.

"I saw her carrying a medicine ball through the parking garage," Margaret said. She turned to Zeno. "Ever do squats with one of those? Or throw them at a target? It makes for a fantastic workout."

"Medicine balls are great tools." He widened his eyes in mock excitement. "I like to do walking lunges while holding one overhead. Real muscle burner."

"This is a conspiracy," Eduardo told them. "I can outrun everyone in this building except the security personnel—and perhaps even a few of them—yet all of you insist I see Greta three times a week."

"It's reassuring to the citizens of San Rimini to know that you are taking steps to protect your health and that your heart is as strong as can be following your surgery," Sergio said. "Besides, you like Greta."

"Not when she's telling me to hold a side plank an extra thirty seconds. I informed her that San Rimini has strict laws against injuring the monarch."

"I'm sure she reminded you that you signed a waiver?" Zeno retorted.

He eyed his press secretary. "She insisted that she wasn't injuring the monarch. *Then* she informed me that it didn't matter because I'd signed a waiver."

Eduardo took a seat at his desk, then thanked Luisa as she reentered the room with a steaming cup of coffee and placed it on a coaster near his hand. When she was gone again, he looked at Sergio. The arrival of Eduardo's first cup of coffee marked the official start of his workday. "Let's discuss the difficult items first. You received a letter over the weekend from the Central District Historical Society?"

"Yes, Your Highness. They have concerns about your desire to upgrade the Strada il Teatro."

"I expected as much, but hoped they would wait until tomorrow's meeting to express them."

"They want to ensure they are heard."

Eduardo resisted the urge to grimace. Everyone wanted to be heard, particularly when it came to making changes to the country's most famous thoroughfare. The Strada il Teatro sat above the country's Adriatic coastline and offered stunning views of San Rimini Bay. It was home to several casinos, restaurants, historic buildings, and the Royal Theater, hence its name as Theater Street. It was the country's most recognizable symbol, aside from the Duomo and the palace itself. However, the last major changes to the street—aside from paving it—took place long before automobiles were commonplace. Traffic often moved at a crawl and the sidewalks were packed with tourists at all hours. Despite the obvious need for refurbishment, San Riminians were protective of its appearance. It was why Sergio had organized a meeting for the following day to present the king's proposal to those most directly affected. He'd invited representatives from the Central District Historical Society, the casino owners' board, the San Rimini Business Council, and the San Rimini Grand Prix organizing committee, together with the country's transportation minister. Sergio had even included those in charge of maintaining the public park that ran below one section of the Strada. Once Sergio had

their input, Eduardo planned to present a comprehensive modernization plan to parliament for their consideration.

As king of San Rimini, Eduardo had more power to affect policy
than monarchs in countries such as Japan or Sweden. He could not
vote, but he had the right to introduce legislation and speak on any
matter under discussion in parliament. In the centuries since San
Rimini had transitioned from an absolute monarchy to a constitu-
tional monarchy, kings and queens primarily exercised their political
might to improve relations with other nations or to promote charitable and humanitarian causes. They steered clear of detailed policy
and budgetary issues.

This piece of legislation would cause many to dig in their heels.
However, Eduardo refused to leave the modernization to his succes-
sors or to members of parliament who feared that touching the Strada
il Teatro meant losing their seats. It was his responsibility to move
San Rimini forward.

Eduardo looked at Sergio. "Inform the head of the Historical
Society that the palace fully intends to pursue these improvements—
make sure you use that word, improvements—to the Strada il Teatro,
as they're in the best interest of the country and to all who hold the
central district close to their hearts. We welcome their input tomorrow, which is why we've scheduled this meeting."

Sergio nodded as he took notes. While Sergio wrote, Zeno said,
"Your Highness, they're likely to argue their case to the press. They'll
note that it isn't in the monarch's usual purview to delve into such
matters."

Eduardo spread his palms on his desk. "As of last week, I understand that the royal family is viewed favorably by nearly eighty
percent of the population."

"Seventy-seven percent, sir."

"Seventy-seven percent. Do you know how many members of
parliament dream of that approval rating? We have the opportunity to
leverage that number for the long-term good of the country. The
Strada has remained essentially the same for hundreds of years. The
fact it was constructed with parades in mind means it's wider than

other streets of its era, but it doesn't accommodate modern usage or the influx of tourism our country has seen. Attendees at the San Rimini Grand Prix are pushing against the fences, which is a safety concern. Either the route will need to change or we will need to limit the crowds. No one wants to make that choice."

"Everyone has their fiefdoms," Sergio pointed out. "The casinos and shop owners don't want their entrances blocked while work is completed. The Historical Society doesn't want to alter the appearance of the street. And while the Grand Prix organizers want a safer route and continued growth, they don't want to risk losing the race for a year or more due to construction."

"Agreed," Eduardo said. "So use tomorrow to show them our redevelopment plan, and use our historical and transportation experts to convince them that our proposal is sound. We've put months of research into this, and we're willing to share all of our findings and to listen to their input as we move forward. Change is difficult, but our citizens need the Strada to function for the long term. If we don't get it through parliament with a seventy-seven percent approval rating, we'll never get it. Now, what else do we need to address?"

Zeno ran through the items he would cover at the weekly press briefing, which mainly involved the king's adult children. Prince Antony had visited an opioid addiction rehabilitation facility over the weekend, and Princess Isabella and her husband, Nick, planned to visit three different schools along the country's northern border to talk with students about San Rimini's medieval history. Nick, a medieval studies professor at the University of San Rimini, had arranged a string of school appearances in recent weeks to interest children in the topic.

When Zeno finished, Sergio said, "Tomorrow night, you are hosting a dinner at which the new American ambassador shall present her credentials. She arrived in country yesterday."

"Claire Peyton," Eduardo said, leaning back in his chair. "I read the briefing last night. She was previously the United States Ambassador to Uganda?"

"Yes. It was expected that she would stay on under the new President, but she was reassigned to San Rimini when Ambassador Cartwright announced his retirement." Sergio paused. "It's not a secret that Rich Cartwright spent his final year or two on cruise control. This will be a change. Given that many in the U.S. State Department consider this an elevation of position, she may wish to prove herself."

"I read about the rural education program she helped institute in Uganda. It looked interesting."

"Yes, Your Highness. She will likely request a meeting in the coming weeks to present it to you and ask for San Rimini's involvement. The American president ran on a campaign that focused heavily on education, so it's a priority for the administration. However, it's ultimately a no go for San Rimini. Parliament might support sending funds, but sending teachers or advisors would be less likely, given current security concerns. Even the funds will be a challenge while we're also trying to push the Strada plan."

Eduardo didn't need time to weigh his priorities. There was no contest. "It's my understanding that parliament will address funding for Central District improvements three months from today. I want our proposal to anchor that discussion. From now until then, that's our focus."

He took a sip of his coffee, then asked Margaret, "Where are we on the Our Place program?"

"The five-year anniversary celebration will take place on Friday at the elementary school on Via Fontana. As Patron, you will speak briefly about the need for early intervention mental health support in schools and highlight the ways that Our Place identifies and assists children without stigmatizing them. I have some statistics on the continued need for the program and on its success. I should have a draft speech to you by Thursday, which you can then adapt to your liking."

"Thank you. That's a visit I look forward to making. Any others?"

Margaret ran through updates on two other charitable organizations the king supported, then provided a follow-up report on an event he'd attended for an animal shelter.

At the same moment Margaret finished her update, Luisa entered the room. "Your ride is waiting, Your Highness. Your tour of the dementia care center begins in twenty minutes."

Eduardo thanked Luisa and stood. Sergio, Zeno, and Margaret stood as well. "Are we finished?"

"One last thing, Your Highness," Zeno said. "There will be questions at today's press briefing regarding your visit to the Duomo this Thursday afternoon. Have you decided whether to deliver any remarks?"

Eduardo felt the corner of his mouth twitch, a dead giveaway to his staff that he was uncomfortable with a topic. It was a tell he could usually control, but this had hit him out of the blue. Somehow, between his morning workout and thoughts about the Strada, he'd forgotten his annual trip to visit his wife's final resting place.

"Next year will be the tenth anniversary of Queen Aletta's death. Given the attention that occasion will draw, I'd prefer to skip the remarks this year and keep the visit low key."

Before Zeno could object, he turned to Luisa and asked, "Do I have any free time this afternoon to see Arturo and Paolo when they get home from school?"

The boys, sons of Prince Federico and his late wife, Lucrezia, were always happy when he appeared at their palace apartment for a visit. He refused to consider whether their smiles were due to his sparkling personality or to the treats he often brought from the kitchen.

"Not today," Luisa said. "They have a school trip to the aquarium and won't return until evening."

"I see. And what about time to see Gianluca?" he asked. Prince Antony and his wife Jennifer's infant son was his newest grandchild. "Does anyone know when the baby sleeps?"

A chorus of *no* and *he doesn't* rose around the room.

"Well, then. Please let Jennifer know that if there's a good time, I'd love to visit. If Gianluca happens to be sleeping, I'll simply watch him sleep."

"You have fifteen minutes free around three-thirty, Your Highness. I'll let her know you'll be available."

He nodded to Luisa, thanked Margaret for the work she was doing on the Our Place speech, then addressed Sergio and Zeno. "You know what to do for the Strada. We have ninety days. Let's improve the country."

"WE'RE ABOUT TO MEET AN ICON."

Claire Peyton's gaze slipped past her personal assistant, Karen Hutchinson, to survey the scene outside the car window. "Either that, Karen, or the husband of one. More likely the latter."

Their plane had touched down two days earlier, but Claire hadn't quite adjusted to the fact that she now lived in the tiny, wealthy southern European country of San Rimini rather than the eclectic Kololo neighborhood of Kampala.

Claire turned her focus to the road, making note of the route the driver followed from the embassy to the palace, but not before gesturing toward banners on the front of a museum proclaiming the return of *Aletta: The Exhibition,* after several years on tour. The blues and purples of the setting sun reflected in the building's glass windows, lending it an ethereal quality.

It seemed appropriate, given the subject of the exhibition: a collection of gowns, jewelry, and other items owned by San Rimini's late queen.

"I'm not so sure," Karen replied. "How many of these tourists will send home souvenirs with images of Queen Aletta, do you think, versus images of the king or his children? King Eduardo has a certain magnetism that's hard to ignore."

"I'd choose anything showing the scenery, myself. It's phenomenal."

Karen made a noise of agreement, then they fell silent, taking in the view.

The glittering strip of casinos and restaurants lining the Strada il Teatro, the long thoroughfare that paralleled San Rimini Bay and the Adriatic Sea beyond, seemed as if it couldn't possibly exist on the same planet as the streets of central Kampala. In Kampala, boda-bodas zipped in and out of rush hour traffic, the riders seemingly oblivious to the risks of their patched-together motorbikes and the chaos that surrounded them. Students, office workers, and sidewalk vendors crammed the sidewalks and occasionally zigzagged through traffic. The sound of car horns was constant.

Here, however, expensive cars crept along the boulevard or idled curbside, discharging passengers in front of the casinos. Couples in evening wear strolled from their hotels toward the Royal Theater, where the marquee announced the evening performance of *La Traviata*. Not far from the theater, the high dome of San Rimini's national cathedral, the Duomo, rose to dominate the hillside.

Old World charm and romance permeated the district, like a fairy tale come to life.

Claire flashed on a memory from when she was fourteen or fifteen years old. She and her friends had gathered around the television in her parents' living room as the future king of San Rimini married Lady Aletta Masciaretti. They'd practically left drool spots on the carpet when Eduardo winked at his bride while slipping the ring on her finger, and Aletta had tried to hide a grin. Claire found it surreal that she'd be face-to-face with King Eduardo diTalora in less than an hour, at the formal ceremony to present her diplomatic credentials.

She tried to tell herself that as popular as His Highness might be, his late wife was the one with true icon status. Libraries, schools, and a wing of the Royal Memorial Hospital were named after Queen Aletta.

Claire was simply in the country for as long as the President desired, to represent the United States and its interests to the best of her ability. To do that, she had to remain focused on the king's position as a politician and as the face of his wealthy country, not on his celebrity status or the way she and her friends had mooned over him as they watched his wedding all those years ago.

The car eased past a knot of well-dressed tourists who stood at the curb waiting for the light. Several carried purchases from trendy boutiques, while others held bags bearing the logo of the country's seaside aquarium. Finally, the driver reached their turn, then threaded his way along the narrow cobblestoned side streets, following the arrows pointing to La Rocca.

"La Rocca di Zaffiro," Karen said, glancing at the sign. "The Sapphire Rock."

"I spent a good chunk of last night reading about its history," Claire said. "The oldest remaining section, the keep, was built at the beginning of the First Crusade to keep watch over the bay. The stone was chosen to blend into the landscape and make it difficult to spot from the water. But when the keep was expanded, a trick of the light at certain times of the day caused the new stone to appear bright blue from the water below."

"I wondered how it got its name. I'd never thought of it as being blue." She craned her neck, but there was no way to see the palace from their position.

"Most of the current palace was built in the sixteenth and seventeenth centuries with a gray stone that looks nothing like the original. But apparently, if you look down on the keep from up in the mountains, you can still see hints of the blue."

"Two minutes to the gate," the driver said, twisting so he could be heard in the back seat.

Claire thanked him. *Showtime.*

Without being asked, Karen held out a compact so Claire could do a quick check of her makeup. Spotting a smudge at the edge of one dark brown eye, she used her pinky to swipe at her eyeliner, then, satisfied, she returned the compact. She adjusted the fabric of her red silk skirt to keep it from wrinkling before their arrival, then checked to ensure the looped buttons down the front of her white silk top remained firmly closed.

No, this was nothing like living in Uganda. She ran a hand over her hair one final time, making sure no strands protruded from the sides of her short cut, then took a deep breath.

As if reading her mind, Karen said, "Your job here will be different than it has been the last five years. You'll actually need to use hairspray and wear formal gowns more than once or twice a year. You'll be working with both the royal family and with parliament."

Claire couldn't quite hide her smile. She always tried to look professional, but she couldn't remember being as concerned with her appearance during her time in Africa. Of course, the cameras hadn't been on her as frequently then, whereas paparazzi were part of the San Riminian landscape. "I had a few gowns shipped from my storage locker in the States. They should arrive in a few days. I just hope I can be as effective here as I was in Uganda. The work we needed to do there was more apparent."

"You can. You have an impeccable reputation and the weight of the U.S. government behind you. And you're *you*. No one stands in the way of Ambassador Claire Peyton."

Claire smiled. Karen always knew the right thing to say. "Thank you for the vote of confidence."

Karen raised her hand, palm out. "Voice of truth."

The car rolled to a stop outside a massive pair of wrought iron gates. After a uniformed guard walked around the vehicle to inspect it, then spoke with the driver, he nodded to another guard. The gates opened, allowing them to enter the palace grounds. Gravel crunched beneath the tires as they skirted the edge of a large garden, then circled to the palace's rear entrance.

As the driver opened the door for them, a lean woman with light brown, shoulder-length hair approached from the wide stone staircase. Her chic beige dress and the confidence with which she walked would have identified her as being a member of the royal family, even if her familiar face didn't.

"Madam Ambassador," the young woman greeted Claire in clear, American English that hearkened to her upbringing outside Washington, D.C. She smiled first at Claire, then at Karen. "I'm Amanda diTalora. It's a pleasure to welcome you to San Rimini. My husband, Prince Marco, looks forward to meeting you when you present your credentials to King Eduardo tonight."

"I look forward to meeting Prince Marco, as well." She gestured to her right. "This is Karen Hutchinson, my personal assistant."

"A pleasure to meet you, Ms. Hutchinson. If you'll accompany me, I'd consider it an honor to give you a quick tour of the palace's public areas before dinner begins."

Claire thanked Amanda, and as she lifted the hem of her long silk skirt to clear the stone steps, she added, "I hope I'm not keeping you from getting ready for dinner. I was told the attire is formal."

"It is, but I can change quite quickly." She gestured toward a group of palace employees gathered nearby and said, "The palace has a large staff who basically run my life so I don't have to. My gown and shoes are being laid out for me as we speak. All I have to do is put my arms and legs in the proper spots."

Amanda dropped her voice so only Claire and Karen could hear. "It takes some getting used to. I worked with children of dignitaries before I married Prince Marco, so even though I spent a great deal of time around wealth, I lived in a tiny studio apartment near Dupont Circle and barely had two dimes to rub together. I considered ramen noodles and tomato soup to be major food groups."

Claire shot Amanda an understanding smile. "You can't imagine how familiar that sounds. When I was in college in New Mexico, word spread like lightning whenever the local grocery had a sale on ramen. I lived on the stuff—well, that and cans of tuna. I hate to think how much sodium I consumed. By the time I moved to Georgetown for graduate school, I was so sick of ramen that I agreed to move into a three-bedroom apartment with five other people. I chose food over privacy."

"Ouch. Georgetown is wonderful, but it's a challenge living there on a student budget."

Amanda took her time guiding Claire and Karen through La Rocca's first floor, stopping to point out each of the historically important rooms and showing the best way to the king's official office, since Claire would likely visit during her tenure. Her manner made Claire instantly comfortable. She suspected that Amanda's easy ability to connect with others explained why she'd become popular with the people of San Rimini, despite being an American.

As they circled back toward the Imperial Ballroom, where the dinner and reception would soon begin, a man wearing a tailored black suit and understated gray tie approached and asked for a moment with Claire to discuss business.

Amanda nodded, then checked her watch and acknowledged that it was time for her to prepare for dinner. To Claire, she explained, "Sergio Ribisi is King Eduardo's top political advisor. I'll allow him to introduce himself, then he'll cover the program for the evening and escort you to the ballroom. I will see you there shortly."

Claire thanked Amanda for taking the time to show her around the palace. Sergio Ribisi shook both Claire and Karen's hands as they made their introductions. To Claire, he said, "It's my pleasure to welcome you to San Rimini, Madam Ambassador. I expect we will continue the strong relationship Ambassador Cartwright worked to build between our two countries. He was quite popular both here and in parliament. He spoke highly of you."

She thanked him for the compliment while Karen took the opportunity to walk to a window a discreet distance down the hall, taking in the view of the garden so Claire could speak to the king's advisor in private.

"How may I help you, Signore Ribisi?"

"Please, call me Sergio."

"Sergio, then. You said you wished to discuss business?"

"Yes, though I'd like to run through the evening's schedule with you first." The rail-thin man proceeded to tick off the order of events for the evening. Everything coincided with the briefing Karen had given her earlier.

As Sergio spoke, Claire studied his face. There were a few lines at the corners of his mouth, as if he held his stress in his jaw. But his eyes were bright, his teeth white and straight, and he had a full head of thick, jet black hair. He was around thirty-five, if she had to guess. She wondered how long he'd been working for the king. He was young to be in the innermost of King Eduardo's circles.

"That sounds straightforward," she said as he wrapped up. "Was there something else?"

"Yes, Madam Ambassador." He hesitated a beat, then said, "Before you arrived, your office sent a letter to mine outlining the issues that you hope to address during your first days here. While most of the items involve furthering diplomatic initiatives discussed by your predecessor and King Eduardo, there was one new item you mentioned that I'd like to discuss."

Claire knew what was coming. She kept a polite smile on her face despite the wave of disappointment that rose in her.

"While you were in Uganda, you worked with the government to institute a regional education program directed at disadvantaged children. It's my understanding that you brought in teachers from the United States, and then from several other nations to work with children."

"That's the core of the program, yes. It started in Uganda but has since expanded to neighborhoods in need in Tanzania, Rwanda, and Burundi. My successor plans to continue the program. It's my belief—and the President's—that when children from rural or poor areas have access to the same educational resources as children in larger urban areas, they're better able to contribute to their economies once they leave school. They aspire to careers once considered beyond their reach. Perhaps in finance, the law, or medicine. We'd even like to see some of those children come back and teach in the program themselves."

"I read the summary report, which was impressive. You've built solid partnerships. You noted in your letter that you planned to continue your support of the program to the extent feasible in your new role here, and that you hoped to discuss the matter with King Eduardo."

Claire chose her words carefully. "San Rimini has an excellent education system and a tradition of providing assistance to its neighbors. I believe involvement in this program could be of great benefit. Even if I had remained in my post in Uganda, I would eventually have contacted your government regarding a potential partnership. Austria and Italy are already contributing funding and sending teachers."

"Yes, your letter mentioned that." The young man straightened slightly, as if needing to shore up his courage before speaking further.

"The king has looked into it, and while he does see the long-term benefits of the program, he doesn't feel it's feasible for San Rimini to offer their financial support or to supply teachers at this time. I wanted to let you know before the ceremony tonight—"

"So I won't lobby the king over dinner?" Claire said, raising an eyebrow. "Without his support, it's unlikely to get far with parliament."

"Yes."

"In other words, he doesn't want to say no in a public place, while the cameras are watching."

Claire assessed the man's silent reaction to her words. She wanted to argue, to explain that she had no intention of approaching the king tonight about any of her proposals, let alone about the education program, but sensed this wasn't the proper moment, nor the proper person.

She smiled, but it was a cold smile. "Thank you, Sergio. I'll take that under advisement."

CHAPTER 2

SERGIO RIBISI BLINKED, apparently debating whether that meant Claire would keep the topic closed. Before he could argue further, she added, "I'm sure that in the years to come, we will discuss a number of programs beneficial to both our countries. My assistant, Karen, has my trust and a solid understanding of the issues. You can contact her for any reason and know it will get to me or to the appropriate person on my staff."

Karen appeared at Claire's side at the same time that voices rose down the hall, in the direction Amanda had been leading them. Sergio took the hint and extended his arm in the direction of the Imperial Ballroom. "I believe it's time to join the party. Shall we?"

As they strode toward the rotunda that fronted the ballroom, Claire tried to stifle her irritation that King Eduardo had dismissed her idea without bothering to discuss it with her himself. The rural education program was the greatest humanitarian achievement of her time in Uganda. She was certain its success was the primary reason the President appointed her to the coveted post in San Rimini. He'd run on a platform of improving the world economy through education and diplomacy whenever possible, rather than through strong-arm trade tactics. The program meant too much to Claire—and to the new President—for her to allow a potential new partner to walk away without giving the plan their full consideration.

The tinkle of glassware reached Claire's ears. They turned a corner and saw guests being shepherded from the rotunda into the ballroom. Opposite the ballroom doors, a grand staircase descended into the rotunda. A guard stood discreetly near the base, while two others occupied positions at the top. She wondered if the stairs led to the family's private apartments.

Sergio paused. "His Highness will join us here momentarily."

She nodded. The plan was for Claire to enter the ballroom along-side the king, then walk to the low dais at the front of the room, where they would be seated for dinner. King Eduardo would be at the center of the table, with Claire to one side. Prince Antony, the eldest of the king's four children, would be on Claire's other side. The current head of parliament and San Rimini's foreign minister would also be seated at the front of the room.

"Thank you, Sergio," Claire said. "I expect it will be a memorable evening."

"I expect so, Madam Ambassador." As he uttered the words, Sergio's gaze slid toward a side door. A large man entered the hallway. He was obviously security, though his suit was as well-tailored as any guest's. The king followed behind him. When he caught sight of Claire, his smile was practiced, but warm.

Sergio bowed his head slightly as the king approached. "Your Highness, may I present the Honorable Claire Peyton, the Ambassador of the United States. Madam Ambassador, may I introduce His Highness, King Eduardo of San Rimini."

Claire shook the king's hand as his political advisor moved to the side. She introduced Karen, who greeted the king before accompanying Sergio into the ballroom. Once Claire and the king were alone with his guard, she said, "La Rocca is beautiful, Your Highness. It's an honor to present my credentials at such an event."

In Uganda, she'd met the President in his office, presented her credentials to the President and Uganda's foreign minister, then posed for a few pictures. She'd worn a professional suit and heels, given a couple quotes to Kampala's news outlets, and had been back at the embassy to begin her role that same day.

This was something else entirely. Not only did the crystal chandeliers and marble floors of La Rocca add a level of glitz that was nowhere to be found in Uganda's government buildings, San Rimini's credential presentation ceremony was far more formal. It involved a slew of VIPs and their spouses in addition to the world-famous monarch.

"We're pleased to have you at the palace, Madam Ambassador. I'm certain our countries will continue our deep friendship on your watch." His eyes shone with sincerity, but she still wondered how much of the smile was for her and how much was out of habit, given the mass of press photographers who awaited them. But as he gave her hand the slightest squeeze, she found herself unable to tear her eyes away from his clear blue ones.

Eduardo diTalora might be a grandfather, but the man carried himself as if he were much younger. Despite having major heart surgery a few years earlier, he was every bit as fit and handsome as when she'd watched his wedding on television. Her stomach did a slow flip, the same way it had when she'd been a young teenager in braces.

Or maybe not the same. As he released her hand, she noted the textures the press could never properly capture: the fine cut of his tuxedo, the smile lines that extended from the outer corners of his eyes, and the subtle shadings of his salt-and-pepper hair. And then there was the charisma. He radiated it.

The cacophony of voices coming from the ballroom quieted in anticipation of their entrance. Claire inhaled and reminded herself that King Eduardo was a man who happened to represent a country. Not a superhero, not an icon.

He gestured toward the ballroom. "Shall we?"

Claire walked alongside him, their footsteps against the marble floor the only sound in the wide hall. The king's guard followed several paces behind them. When they reached the ballroom doors, a tuxedoed man standing just inside the room announced, "His Highness, King Eduardo of San Rimini, and the Honorable Claire Peyton, Ambassador of the United States."

Inside the ballroom, all stood. There was a momentary pause, then to one side of the ballroom, a group of musicians from the Royal Orchestra began to play "Guardian of the Adriatic." She'd listened to it earlier that day to familiarize herself with the tune. Its lyrics spoke to the beauty of San Rimini and the strength of its people, united in purpose under a vigilant monarch.

"It's a beautiful melody," Claire whispered as they waited for the note that would signal the time for them to walk.

"I've always thought so," he replied. "Most of Europe copied 'God Save the Queen,' which itself was copied from the French. Our composers went their own way."

If she thought the king had charisma while they stood in the hallway, it doubled in its intensity as the music swelled and they entered the room. And she wasn't the only one to notice. Every eye locked on the man beside her.

Eduardo cast a welcoming smile to his guests and instantly the mood became more festive, despite the formality of the moment. Claire marveled at his talent for making each of the two hundred guests feel as if he'd meant the smile specifically for them. Clearly, he'd had a lifetime of practice making a grand entrance.

"The orchestra will transition into something American and patriotic to welcome you," he said, leaning close to her and speaking quietly as they moved through the room. "I, for one, will be grateful. As beautiful as our anthem may be, I hear it often enough to be tired of it."

"I somehow doubt that," she replied. "'Hail to the Chief' never seems to get old to American presidents or military bands."

"Your President serves eight years at the most. That's just enough time for the song to run its course in their heads. On the other hand, I imagine that at some point every British monarch has thought, 'please stop asking God to save me. Your request has been heard by now.'"

"But your anthem is the perfect balance of catchy and stately. And so very San Riminian."

"That it is."

Claire moved slowly, smiling at the guests as she and the king circled toward the dais. She recognized several as embassy employees. Others were members of key government departments or held seats in San Rimini's parliament. She caught sight of Karen, who gave her a discreet nod of approval that put her at ease. She was grateful to have such a reliable and capable woman on her team. As the evening wore on, Karen would move through the room, picking out the individuals Claire needed to make a point of greeting. She'd introduce herself, familiarize herself with their issues, and ensure various embassy departments were notified of anyone who wished to speak at greater length about American business interests, programs, or government policies.

It was a celebratory evening, but a working one.

Within a few minutes, everyone was seated and enjoying a selection of local specialties. Prince Antony turned out to have a dry sense of humor, which kept Claire entertained as they ate. When dinner was nearly finished, the crown prince stood to quiet the room and thank everyone for sharing in the evening's events, then the ceremony began. Claire presented her letter of credence from the President, then King Eduardo spoke briefly about his pleasure at meeting a new ambassador before stating that he anticipated building upon U.S.-San Riminian relations.

Then it was Claire's turn. She thanked the guests for offering her a warm welcome to San Rimini, noting that the country would make a wonderful home and that she looked forward to learning all she could about its residents and their traditions. But as her eyes scanned the speech she'd written earlier that week and she said all the usual niceties about her desire to improve trade relations, address environmental concerns, and boost tourism between their two nations, her gaze lit on one word: education. That was all she'd written, a single word. Suddenly, that single word didn't feel sufficient.

She looked up from the lectern, taking in the faces of the crowd. "Finally, as many of you know, I've come here after spending two years at the American embassy in Cairo, followed by five years working in Kampala, Uganda." A few murmurs floated through the room, and she added, "Yes, this is quite a change. There are many in this world who face poverty that can be difficult for us to imagine while dining in this beautiful building or while enjoying our daily lives with the benefits of a stable government, one that you have worked for centuries to create and preserve here in San Rimini."

She allowed her gaze to encompass several members of parliament, then turned to look at King Eduardo. His eyes held an unexpected challenge and she had to force herself not to look away. What was it about this man? His title? His reputation? Claire had never in her life been intimidated by anyone. Her mother had been raised in a household with spotty electricity, in an area where the chance to receive a full education was beyond the reach of many families, yet her mother had succeeded in life, and she'd told her children from the day they were born to take advantage of every opportunity presented to them, and to fight hard to pursue their dreams.

Well, this was Claire's dream.

In a level voice, she said, "Education is the key to all that San Rimini is today. King Eduardo has been a great supporter of equal access to education, as were his predecessors. That support has translated into a high standard of living for all San Riminians."

She shifted her focus to the larger audience. "Your elected officials have also been enthusiastic supporters of your educational system. You have solid programs that begin with the youngest students, while the University of San Rimini is known around the world for its cutting-edge research and scholarly exploration. The opportunities it offers are a source of pride for many of your citizens. It is my hope that the United States can work hand in hand with San Rimini to make similar opportunities available to those who aren't as fortunate."

Claire paused. She itched to say more, even knowing it was a knee-jerk reaction to Sergio Ribisi telling her in no uncertain terms not to push the issue. But as she'd spoken, she'd caught a vibe from the king that made her realize she'd have better luck if she stopped now, having said just enough to make her point, but without saying so much that the audience would suspect there'd already been friction between their monarch and the new American ambassador.

She glanced at her notes, found her closing paragraph on the benefits of international friendship and cooperation, and finished with it. She returned to her seat to a good deal of applause, including King Eduardo's. However, she could tell from his body language that she'd been right to take her shot at the lectern, because she wouldn't get another.

And with any luck, tonight's shot wouldn't ricochet.

SERGIO RIBISI'S jaw twitched as he leaned toward Eduardo and pitched his voice so others couldn't hear. "I spoke with Ambassador Peyton before dinner, Your Highness. I apparently failed to make my point. Ambassador Cartwright would have understood. Next time, I'll be blunt."

King Eduardo shook his head. "It's not a concern, Sergio. The ambassador's speech was prepared. She may not have been comfortable going off script at the last moment. No harm done."

He glanced across the room to where Claire Peyton spoke with a group that included his daughter Isabella and his son Marco, as well as several members of parliament and an American telecommunications executive. She appeared confident, but at ease. He had to admire her for sticking to her convictions, even if she wouldn't get her way in the long run.

While Eduardo had liked Ambassador Cartwright personally, the man hadn't wanted to make waves as he neared retirement, so his work had centered on uncontroversial issues. He'd relished his posh station and didn't want to risk losing it or being reassigned to a country without a beautiful, historical ambassador's home like that provided in San Rimini, where he had easy access to theaters, fine dining, and an active social scene.

Somewhere like Uganda.

"The orchestra is preparing to play," Sergio continued. "I'd like to follow up on something with the transportation minister before the dancing begins and it becomes difficult to speak."

Eduardo nodded. "I know you'll brief everyone tomorrow on how the development meeting went, but what was the overall result?"

"We have a challenge ahead of us, but I'm optimistic."

That was music to Eduardo's ears. Sergio didn't express optimism unless it was warranted. "Best of luck with the transportation minister, then."

Sergio excused himself and Eduardo took the opportunity to speak with a member of parliament he'd known for nearly twenty years. Behind the parliamentarian, one of the Royal Orchestra members signaled Prince Antony that they were ready to begin. Eduardo was grateful that Antony and Jennifer would lead the guests on the dance floor. In recent years, Eduardo did his best to avoid the dancing that was expected at so many formal events. As a widower, and as king of his country, he had to be careful about who he chose as a partner on such occasions. Someone single and high on the social ladder prompted tabloid talk that they were romantic partners. If the woman had even a hint of scandal in her past, that hit the tabloids too, with subtle digs about his judgment. The media could take pieces of a person's life and spin them to tell a story that was the polar opposite of the truth. It galled him that a short dance and idle conversation could draw attention away from all the positive work either he or his dance partner might be doing.

As the music started, the crown prince led his wife to the dance floor. A moment later, Marco and his wife, Amanda, joined them, bringing along an American entrepreneur and her husband.

The harsh glare of the media spotlight alternated between Eduardo and his four children, but always seemed to return to him and the question of his status as a wealthy, royal widower. On nights like this, where the press scurried around the room searching more intently for gossip than for hard news, he told himself it could be worse. He could be a Windsor. The attention garnered by the arrival of a new ambassador in San Rimini was nothing when compared to formal events at Buckingham Palace.

He concluded his discussion with the parliamentarian, then turned to accept a glass of sparkling water from a passing waiter.

His country was at peace, he was happily productive, and though each of his four adult children lived their own lives, they'd chosen to remain under the same roof at La Rocca, allowing him to spend time with them and his three grandsons as he desired.

If he had to deal with ballrooms and dancing every so often, it was a small price to pay.

"You find something on the dance floor amusing, Your Highness? Or is there humor in the choice of music?"

He turned to see Claire Peyton standing beside him, wineglass in hand. The top of her dark head just reached his shoulder. Apparently, she'd caught him smiling to himself as he'd been lost in a moment of contemplation. "Actually, I was thinking about my children. It's rare that we all attend the same event."

"I understand why that would make you smile." She looked toward the center of the floor, where Princess Isabella and her husband had joined the others. "From what I've seen, you and your wife raised four good human beings. That must have been a challenge, given the spotlight."

"We certainly had our moments, but they're happy, and that's what counts. What about you? Partner? Children?"

"No. Brief marriage and divorce long ago."

She said it plainly, as if she'd answered the question a thousand times. She likely had. She didn't seem bothered by it.

He couldn't help but smile at her. Claire Peyton was a marked change from the previous ambassador. Her eyes sparkled as she spoke, as if she were fully engrossed in every conversation, not only with him, but with others as well. Her speech had been eloquent, the perfect length, and—he suspected—partially off the cuff, despite what he'd told Sergio. Her dark brown hair was short and professional, though it curled around her ears in a way he found sexy. On the other hand, Rich Cartwright was pushing seventy-five during his stint as ambassador, wore perpetually rumpled suits and sported a short gray buzz cut. And though Rich had exceptional diplomatic skills,

Eduardo suspected Claire would be more engaged than Rich had been.

"What is it?"

His face heated at having been caught staring. It took him a second to recover. "Oh, nothing. I was wondering why you thought I might find humor in the orchestra's selection."

Her brows lifted at that. "Do you recognize it?"

He listened, then shook his head. "I've heard it before, but don't know the name. It's beautiful."

"It's called 'Let the Rest of the World Go By.' Willie Nelson sang a popular version. But this is a different one, an arrangement by John Barry that was featured in the movie *Out of Africa*."

He looked at her in surprise. "Ah. I see why you might find the choice amusing. I doubt anyone has made the connection to your last assignment."

"It would be a stretch. But yes, it amused me." A soft smile hovered on her lips as she watched the musicians. "It's actually one of my favorite pieces. Have you seen the movie?"

"Years ago. I'm afraid I don't remember much of it."

She took a slow sip of her wine, then said, "There's a point in the film where the main character, Karen Blixen, is forced to sell all her belongings. Furniture, artwork, even her mother's dishes. Everything she has collected over a lifetime in Denmark and Kenya. It was stacked outside her farmhouse one night, ready for a rummage sale the next morning. She sat in her empty house, eating dinner off the top of a packing crate." Claire raised a hand, gesturing at an imaginary house as she spoke. "You could feel her misery and sense of failure, that this woman who'd worked so hard was about to lose the sum total of her life. Robert Redford's character, Denys, entered the house. The sight of her gutted him. She told him that when things were bad, she tried to make them worse in her head. When she did that, she knew she could withstand anything. She asked if he would help her. When he nodded, she turned to her gramophone, which was sitting nearby, and put on this song. They danced through the empty house, then into the front yard, through the middle of all her belongings. By the end, they were both smiling." Claire's own smile broadened a notch. "It was a message about valuing experiences and people over things. To focus on the moment and let the rest of the world go by. At least, that was the message I took from it."

"You make me want to watch the movie again and pay better attention."

"It's one of those rare movies worth a rewatch." She took a final sip of her wine as the song ended and the orchestra transitioned to a new tune. A waiter materialized to take her glass and offer her another. She declined, then discreetly smoothed her bright red skirt. She had a unique look. Her wide eyes were framed by dark lashes and thick brows. She had smooth olive skin and the kind of full lips that other women paid plastic surgeons scandalous amounts to copy. He wondered what her background might be—if she spoke any languages besides English, where her personal politics centered, if she had any hobbies—and told himself he'd ask Sergio tomorrow. Sergio always seemed to have that kind of information at his fingertips, and Eduardo found he wanted to know more about Claire than what had come from the briefing materials that had been prepared for him.

"Your Highness, it's probably a terrible breach of etiquette—all right, I know this is a breach of etiquette—but I have a question."

"Of course. You may ask anything." He set his water glass on a nearby tray as she glanced toward Isabella and Nick, who were now leaving the dance floor to talk to a group of guests.

In that moment, he knew what she was going to ask. He spoke before she could. "Madam Ambassador, were you planning to ask me to dance?"

CHAPTER 3

HE COULDN'T POSSIBLY HAVE SAID what she thought she heard. Could he?

"Your Highness?" Claire forced herself not to take a step back or to allow the space between her brows to crease into a frown, as she knew it frequently did when she heard something unbelievable.

He extended his elbow toward her. "Would you care to dance?"

So he *had* said it. Clearly, she had a lot to learn about how things worked in San Rimini.

"I'd be honored."

His mouth rose into an odd half-smile as she placed her hand on his arm and allowed him to lead her toward the center of the room, where most of the other guests now spun under the crystal chandeliers.

It made sense, she supposed. Usually the host at events like this would dance with the guest of honor or the guest's spouse. But somehow, it'd never crossed her mind that she was expected to dance with the king. Karen had never mentioned it. Nor had Sergio Ribisi when he ran over the schedule of events with her, and he'd been quite detailed.

Somewhere in the back of her mind, she wondered if her family would read about this tomorrow. They'd always been proud of her and knew she worked hard at her job, but this was the first time she'd been around the glitterati of southern Europe, let alone royalty, and she knew her parents would find the press coverage exciting.

Claire smiled to herself, amused at the track her mind had taken out of self-defense. Focusing on her family kept her attention off what she was actually doing: dancing with a king. A very handsome, technically eligible king. One with bright blue eyes, a warmer personality than she'd expected, and a smile that could enthrall an entire room—and would do so whether or not he was king.

But he *was* a king, one she'd have to negotiate with on a regular basis over the coming months and years. One who could stand between her and her goals...or give those goals wings.

He turned her gently, then rested one hand on her lower back and guided her around the floor. His steps were smooth and sure, and she wondered how much time he'd spent as a child learning to handle formal events—how to dance, what to say, how to eat—in a manner appropriate for a king.

"I'm now convinced the *Out of Africa* choice was entirely coincidental," Eduardo said, slipping a look in the direction of the musicians. "This song has no deep meaning whatsoever. It's a number. Composition number five or nine or some such. I'm certain I had to identify it for a music teacher when I was younger, but I've conveniently allowed that knowledge to drift away."

"I can't identify it at all, so you're ahead of me."

She expected him to continue engaging in pleasantries. Instead, a quick grimace flashed across his face. "You weren't going to ask me to dance, were you, Madam Ambassador?"

"No, I wasn't." She surprised herself by her candid answer, at the same time she was embarrassed by the fact he'd made that assumption, then invited her onto the dance floor himself to save her from making a faux pas. "And...I suspect I just made this awkward."

His laugh was quick and genuine. "In addressing it, you just removed the awkwardness. Well done."

"I'm a diplomat. It's what I do. At least if I do my job correctly."

"I see." They took a few more steps around the center of the floor before he asked, "Then what were you planning to ask that you felt would be a breach of etiquette?"

She took a moment to consider her words as they spun closer to Antony and Jennifer, then away again, nearer to one of the king's security guards, who moved along the periphery of the dancing area, discreetly watching the crowd. "I know we're not here to talk specifics on politics and policy—"

"True."

"But I wanted to ask you about something your advisor, Sergio Ribisi, mentioned to me earlier this evening."

The soft lines of his forehead deepened a notch. "Did he say something to offend you?"

"No, but he did catch me off guard." She met the king's curious gaze. "I wasn't expecting to be told which matters I should or should not speak to you about this evening."

He took a moment to process that. "You're referring to the education program you worked on in Uganda?"

"Yes."

They quieted momentarily as a palace photographer came close for a picture. When she retreated, Claire said, "Your Highness, I didn't intend to discuss the plan—or anything policy-related—in detail tonight. Tonight is about the ceremony itself and the opportunity for me to meet you and some of the key personnel on your staff and in parliament. It's also a chance for your government officials to evaluate what kind of ambassador I'll be and how we might best work together."

"Then I fear it is I who have offended you, rather than Sergio."

"Not at all, Your Highness. Slighted, perhaps, but I'm not one to take offense when none was intended."

She angled her head for a better look at him. The king was taller than she'd expected, and she was in heels. "However, when we have our first official meetings, I would like to discuss the education program, along with other social and economic policy initiatives that are relevant to San Rimini. Our countries have a long history of cooperation, and I believe that working together on these projects will only deepen the relationship between us."

The relationship between our countries, she clarified in her head. Next time, she'd be more careful in her phrasing.

"I'm sure we will find our points of agreement, Madam Ambassador."

His hand shifted slightly against her lower back, but the spot where his hand had been remained warm from his touch. Claire had danced with foreign officials more than once, but for some reason, dancing with King Eduardo felt different. There was a gravitas to the moment she wasn't certain how to interpret.

"Have you moved into the ambassador's residence?"

"Next week. Ambassador Cartwright's belongings are scheduled to ship out the day after tomorrow."

"And after that, I assume it will be cleaned and a fresh security sweep conducted?"

"That's the routine. My belongings are still in transit from Uganda, so there's no rush."

"You'll find the diplomatic community here is very tight-knit. Most embassies are within a few blocks of each other, as are the ambassadors' residences. Richard Cartwright loved the sense of camaraderie that created. He also mentioned on more than one occasion how much he'd miss the house itself. He'd put off retirement for several years longer than he originally planned in order to accept the position in San Rimini, despite the fact his children and grandchildren are in California."

"I wasn't in town in time for the farewell party at the residence, but I understand it was quite the event. He told me that leaving after such an incredible night was bittersweet."

Eduardo smiled at that. "I didn't attend, but my daughter, Isabella, was there. He told her the same thing."

The music grew louder for a moment as the song reached its crescendo. The king waited for the volume to drop, then said, "Isabella hadn't been inside the residence since before its renovation. She tells me it was beautifully done."

"It was. Ambassador Cartwright gave me a tour and showed me several 'before' pictures. It's stunning what was accomplished. The architect and construction crew took care to honor the home's history. They brought the plumbing and electrical systems to modern standards, but used period fixtures. When you walk through, it feels as if you're inside the original home."

"It's one of the oldest in the area, isn't it?"

She nodded. "It was built by a shipping company owner in the early seventeenth century. His great-great-grandson had no children, so he willed it to a teacher, who opened a school for girls in the late 1700s. She lived on the top floor and the girls lived below. It operated out of the home for nearly a hundred years, when other facilities became available and the school was shuttered. A decade or so later, it was purchased by the U.S. government and refurbished. This was its first major renovation since then. I'm looking forward to exploring its nooks and crannies. Who knows what secrets it holds?"

The king laughed, which drew the attention of several people nearby. Claire was surprised that it sounded so...so *human*. It wasn't the laugh of a celebrity who knew his every word and utterance was being scrutinized. Rather, it was the type of laugh one heard between friends. One of appreciation.

In the time since he'd greeted her in the rotunda, he'd lost the gloss of self-awareness. Given his position, it was likely temporary, but she liked seeing him this way.

"In that case, I have a feeling you'll enjoy the home for different reasons than Ambassador Cartwright did. I believe he valued its location more than anything else. It's close to the Strada il Teatro and the nightlife."

"I understand the allure of the theater, but I'm a terrible gambler. The ability to walk to a casino is wasted on me."

"No one could be in your position without gambling skills. But I do agree with you about the home. I've always had a fondness for old books and the collection in the ambassador's residence is impressive." A sparkle—either from amusement, or from the chandeliers overhead

—lit the king's eyes. "I suspect you're the type who enjoys a good book."

"I am. I'm looking forward to seeing what's on the shelves." His hand shifted on her back, sending another zing of heat along her spine and distracting her, though she recovered enough to say, "It sounds as if you're familiar with the home's interior."

"I attended a dinner party there shortly after Ambassador Cartwright came to San Rimini, and we met in the library on a few occasions. It was easier than meeting at the embassy or here in the palace if we had sensitive issues to discuss. I haven't seen it since the renovation, though."

She tried to focus on his words, rather than on the way his rich voice and San Riminian accent wrapped around her. Unfortunately, that didn't help. She was left with a mental picture of King Eduardo sitting near the fireplace in what was now her library, his feet on the plush ottoman, chatting about the issues of the day. She wondered if he'd be more relaxed outside the palace, away from public scrutiny.

The song was nearing its end, so she took her shot. "In that case, you'll have to come see it and let me know what you think of the changes. Perhaps when we meet to discuss our mutual goals."

"I would like that." She felt the seriousness descend over him before he continued speaking. "I did take a few minutes to look into your education program. I admire its success. However, I don't believe it's feasible for San Rimini to participate at this time."

Another couple moved within hearing distance. She waited until she was certain they weren't listening to speak. "I appreciate your candor. However, would you at least allow me the opportunity to present it to you myself? It deserves more than a few minutes' consideration. The President would appreciate it if you heard me out, whether or not you decide to support it."

The music slowed, the song fading as another began. The king guided her off the dance floor and toward the tables. A man in his mid-thirties wearing a navy suit and sky blue tie approached, his manner one of someone with information to share. Before Eduardo took his leave, however, he turned to Claire. "I'll consider it, Madam Ambassador. And thank you for not asking me to dance."

He delivered the last bit with a quick wink that caught Claire by surprise. Before she could respond, the king was pulled aside, then steered toward a group standing near the door that included two high-ranking members of parliament. No doubt some pressing issue had arisen, though Claire suspected it was no emergency. The king didn't appear as if he needed to leave.

"That was interesting." Karen materialized at Claire's side. She carried a glass of sparkling water in each hand and offered one to Claire. "I was told the king rarely dances at these events. You must be working your magic."

A laugh escaped Claire as she accepted the glass. "More like courting disaster. He asked me to dance because he misunderstood something I said."

Karen's mouth twisted. "Is that good or bad?"

"I'm not certain yet." She glanced toward the king and noticed that his discussion was already breaking up.

"The good-looking guy with the light blue tie and dark hair is the king's liaison to the defense ministry," Karen said, her gaze following Claire's. "There was a traffic accident in front of one of the casinos on the Strada il Teatro. Parliament and the king are briefed whenever something like that occurs in a key location so they know that it was truly an accident, rather than a terrorist threat."

"Must have been bad."

"Apparently a driver braked hard for a pedestrian, which caused a series of rear-end crashes. No serious injuries that I've heard of, but it shut down the road and sidewalk for several blocks. We'll have to take a different route back."

Claire took a long sip of her drink, grateful for a break in the evening's events. As much as she enjoyed her job, she wasn't used to socializing on the level that would be required of her now that she was in San Rimini. Her head was starting to throb.

"I was approached by two of King Eduardo's economic advisers," Karen said. "They asked for a meeting with you, preferably in the next two to three weeks, so you can discuss the trade initiatives Rich Cartwright was working on. I told them that I'm happy to make arrangements, but didn't commit to a date. Since you were dancing with His Highness at the time and it looked like the two of you were having quite the conversation, I'd hoped—"

If there hadn't been people watching, Claire would have scowled. "You'd hoped what?"

"I'd like to leave some free time in your calendar, in case you do get a chance to present your education program." A wicked glint entered her eye. "You lobbied him while you were dancing, didn't you?"

"I told him I'd appreciate the opportunity to present it before having it dismissed out of hand. Don't hold your breath, though. As much as I want his support, it isn't our only matter of business. If other meetings can be arranged, go ahead."

"Understood."

Claire shot a look toward the king and realized he was looking at her, too. His brilliant blue eyes locked with hers, and she fought the urge to turn away and pretend she hadn't seen him watching her.

"On second thought, maybe I should leave a spot or two open," Karen said, hiding her words behind the glass she held to her lips. "You keep working your magic."

"It's business, Karen. Don't even think about hinting otherwise."

"I wouldn't dream of it, Madam Ambassador."

"This from the same woman who used the phrase 'good looking' to describe a defense ministry liaison before using 'light blue tie' or 'dark hair.'"

"Good looking is a defining characteristic," she protested.

"A blue tie is the same to everyone. Good looking is in the eye of the beholder."

"In this case, it was accurate."

A member of San Rimini's state department approached and they moved to professional topics, but as Karen looked at Claire over the rim of her glass, a devilish smile remained in her eyes.

CHAPTER 4

EDUARDO COULDN'T BELIEVE he'd winked at Claire Peyton at the end of their dance. Not only was it inappropriate, it was the first overtly flirtatious thing he'd done in years. It hadn't been calculated; he'd just done it.

He'd winked at an ambassador.

Thankfully, he'd been standing an angle that ensured no one else witnessed his lapse in judgment or he'd be hearing about it from his chief political advisor at this very moment.

Sergio occupied one of the two striped silk sofas opposite Eduardo's desk in the palace office. Eduardo sat behind the desk, leaning over its large mahogany work surface as he made his final edits on a speech he was scheduled to give that night at the War Museum of San Rimini. When he caught himself scribbling through a line with red pencil and simultaneously deciding it was perfect the way it was, he took off his reading glasses and looked up. He was used to working on speeches with Sergio in the room, but for some reason, the advisor's presence distracted him today.

No, it was the wink that distracted him. He'd rather blame Sergio. Or Zeno. The press secretary had been in and out of the office three times in the last forty minutes, checking on progress. The man was as single-minded as a lion stalking prey when it came to knowing the content of Eduardo's speeches. But again, that was part of his routine.

Eduardo swore inwardly. Winking at the new ambassador was only part of the problem. He'd also offended her by having Sergio run interference on her education plan, even if she claimed not to have taken offense. Claire Peyton had been right: he should have heard her out before dismissing her plan entirely.

But he would dismiss it. Entirely. Last night's accident on the Strada il Teatro was another reminder of the project's importance. Three people had required ambulance transport following the initial crash, and a five-hundred-year-old building sustained damage when a driver behind the accident veered to avoid the smashed cars in front of him. It was a miracle no one on the sidewalk had been hit. It was a second miracle that all those injured had been released from the hospital before the sun rose.

On the other hand, the accident itself surprised no one. Too many pedestrians and too many drivers in a confined area made safety a constant concern. It was made worse because their attention was drawn from the roadway by the casino lights, the spires of the Duomo, and the panoramic view of San Rimini Bay.

Eduardo needed to get both the country's political forces and its historical guardians on his side to accomplish his goal. Now was the time.

"Is something wrong, Your Highness?"

Eduardo shook his head, then pushed the speech across his desk. "I'll go with this version. The section about my sworn duty to preserve our country's history is better than in the original draft."

Sergio picked up the paper, scanned it, then made a low murmur of approval. "Good thought. I'll have Luisa make a clean copy for you and another for Zeno so he's ready for any media questions tomorrow."

"When you talk to Luisa, would you have her come in here, please?"

Sergio nodded, leaving the office with the speech in hand. Eduardo made a quick check of his phone messages, then typed a quick note to his daughter about a photo he saw from the school visit she and Nick had done the previous day. A moment later, Luisa entered, schedule in hand.

"Your Highness?"

He waved toward the device as she tapped its screen. "You won't need that, Luisa. This is just a quick task. I'd like you to send a bouquet to Claire Peyton's office."

She hesitated, but to her credit, recovered quickly. "She's the new American ambassador, correct?"

"Yes. Now that the formalities are complete, she should be in her embassy office. If you could arrange for a delivery this afternoon?"

At Luisa's inquisitive look, he added, "Oh, yes, the card. I'll leave the niceties up to you—welcome to San Rimini, that it was a pleasure to have her and her personal assistant at La Rocca—whatever you think is appropriate. Then state that I'd be happy to arrange a meeting at her convenience to discuss her goals."

Luisa made a quick note. "When her office calls, where should I schedule the appointment? Here, or at the embassy? And how much time will you need? Thirty minutes?"

"Here is fine. Wait, no, on second thought, scratch that." He frowned. He needed the proper venue so the ambassador would feel she'd been heard. However, he didn't want to be trapped listening to an expanded presentation on a project he couldn't seriously consider in the near future.

Luisa interrupted his internal debate. "I'll speak with Ambassador Peyton's office about arranging the meeting there. I assume they're reorganizing the embassy's office space with Ambassador Cartwright's departure, but there should be a meeting room available—"

"No, hold on." He raised one hand in a silent request for time to think. This shouldn't be complicated. He'd made a minor political mistake in cutting off the ambassador's pitch. Such mistakes happened as often with him as with any other government official. It could be remedied quickly enough. It was simply a matter of learning her personality and finding the rhythm of their political relationship.

And not winking at her.

"Scratch the whole card, Luisa. I'll write one myself. I assume I'm still clear tomorrow after six p.m.?"

"As of now, Your Highness."

"All right. Pencil in the ambassador and I'll include a dinner invitation in the card. If she can't make dinner on such short notice, I'd appreciate it if you'd make other arrangements with her office."

A flash of surprise registered on Luisa's face, but she hid it by quickly consulting her schedule...the one he'd told her she wouldn't need. "Prince Marco is hosting an event in the formal dining room tomorrow evening. The garden terrace is a possibility, but rain is expected around seven. Let me see what else might be available."

"My apartment should be fine. Richard Cartwright was there for dinner last year. I'll have Samuel and his staff make the preparations. Is he on duty tomorrow?"

Luisa's eyes widened briefly, but she kept her focus on the schedule in her hand. "He is. Any special requests for the meal?"

"Whatever Samuel feels is best." Samuel Barden, his longtime private chef, was happiest when given latitude to create meals based on what he found at the market on any given day. Eduardo had learned long ago to let Samuel do exactly that.

"Yes, Your Highness. I'll get right on it."

"Thank you. If you could also confirm the transportation to the War Museum for tonight, then I'm set for now."

He expected her to leave, but instead, she asked, "While I'm on the phone with the florist, what would you like for the Duomo?"

It took him a beat to follow. Once again, the visit had slipped his mind. "A dozen white roses, assuming they're available. They were her favorite. If not, then red."

"Shall I have them waiting for you in the sanctuary, or in the car?"

"The car, please. I'd prefer to carry them inside so I can place them myself."

Luisa nodded and turned to go just as Zeno entered the office, causing a near-collision in the doorway. Once he and Luisa muttered their apologies, Zeno asked, "You were talking about your Duomo visit, Your Highness?"

"Yes."

"I know you'd prefer not to make remarks, but something brief might be in order."

Eduardo leaned back in his chair and gave his press secretary a long look. "Let me guess. You received an interview request?"

"Several, but two specifically in regard to the anniversary. One from *San Rimini Today* and one from Val Dempsey at *Today's Royals*. The latter can be skipped. She's always angling for an interview and no matter what you say, she'll give her piece the slant she wants to run. *San Rimini Today* requires more delicate handling."

"Would a few words on the steps of the Duomo be sufficient?"

"If you make a brief statement, I can easily tell both outlets—and anyone else who asks for an interview—that this is a personal occasion and that you'd prefer to limit your statements to what you say outside."

"Have my children received any requests?"

"Yes, all of them. Their offices referred the requests to me. They'd rather follow your lead."

"All right. Put off what you can until tomorrow. I'll prepare something to say as I leave the Duomo."

"If you'd like me to review your remarks, I'm available, Your Highness."

"That won't be necessary." At the big man's look of consternation, Eduardo added, "I know, I know. Every word will be picked apart. I'll keep it brief and make sure I don't repeat what I've said in previous years."

Eduardo stood, tucked a file under his arm, then escorted Zeno out of the office. "Sergio and I finished the edits on tonight's speech for the War Museum. Luisa should have a copy to you shortly."

Mollified, Zeno wished Eduardo good luck at the War Museum before leaving for his own office.

Luisa was on the phone when Eduardo reached her desk, but was apparently on hold. She lowered the receiver and looked at him.

"If anyone needs me, I'll be working in my apartment for the next few hours."

"You'll get the card to me shortly?"

At his nod, she said, "I'll call if anything urgent arises," then shifted the receiver as the person on the other end came on the line.

Within a few minutes, Eduardo entered his apartment, strode to his private study, and toed off his shoes. It had been a long day and he had several things to do before his War Museum appearance. On late afternoons when his energy flagged, this was where he retreated whenever possible. He drew a sense of peace and order from the room's familiar keepsakes and the smell of its floor-to-ceiling bookcases. Better yet, few people interrupted him here, which allowed him to focus.

The file he carried contained a briefing on his upcoming trip to South America. Rather than open it, he dropped it on the desktop and leaned forward, planting his knuckles on either side of the file and closing his eyes. He allowed himself five long breaths, then straightened, resolved to get to work.

Before he could sit, his gaze snagged on the framed photo of Aletta he kept on the corner of his desk. It had been taken as they'd emerged from the Duomo following their wedding ceremony.

"Can you believe it's been nine years?" he asked her image. "You'd hate the way the press makes a yearly production out of your death. You'd have something witty to say about it. Something morbid and hilarious and completely unfit to print."

He reached past the photo to pick up a smaller one he'd taken during an official visit to Spain the year before she'd passed away, before they'd realized her exhaustion was more than a result of her overbooked schedule. They'd had a few minutes alone in Madrid's Campo del Moro park. Aletta was walking in front of him and had stopped to look at a curled leaf on a tree. He'd captured the image just as she'd reached for the leaf, a smile brightening her face at having discovered a caterpillar inside.

In some ways, it seemed as if they'd taken that trip just a few weeks ago. He could still remember how she'd jumped when the caterpillar moved from the leaf to her hand. In other ways, it seemed like an event from another lifetime, as if he'd watched from far away as two other people lived the experience.

Aletta's condition had deteriorated rapidly and the end came earlier than any of them had expected. The night she'd passed away, Antony had been in Africa on a diplomatic mission. Federico and Lucrezia had just married and were in New Zealand on their first state visit. Isabella had been in her final semester of university in London. She'd wanted to come home, but stayed to graduate at Aletta's insistence, though she'd called nearly every night and flew home more weekends than not.

Only Eduardo and Marco had been at the palace on that final, painful night. Marco had started at Princeton the previous fall. He'd entered with a number of credits and had taken a heavy load his first semester, then took off the spring semester to stay in San Rimini. The situation hadn't been easy for any of them and Eduardo still wasn't sure whether Aletta's rapid decline was a blessing or a curse. There were times he wondered how he and his children ever managed to get through the intensity of those days and the massive state funeral that followed.

Somehow, they had. Now all four children were grown and thriving in their royal roles. Federico and Antony had children of their own. He suspected Isabella and Marco, each recently married, also planned to start families soon.

His children's lives had changed drastically in nine years. Yet he'd remained the same. Working to improve his country's economy, promoting charitable causes, attending events late into the night, and then rising again at dawn to go for a run—or to work out with Greta the taskmaster—so he could be back in his office right after breakfast to begin again.

Or...perhaps he wasn't the same.

He couldn't look at the picture of Aletta in Spain without feeling as if she'd been frozen at that age. The shining, beautiful woman who smiled at the caterpillar no longer looked like someone he could banter with at the end of a long day, someone with the wisdom and maturity to understand the complexities of his life. Close, but not quite. They'd married young, and for many years they had grown and learned together.

Then they hadn't.

A pang of guilt grabbed his gut at the stunning thought that, in the last decade, he'd outgrown his own wife.

Deep down, he'd known it for some time, but today it hit him with more clarity. He shoved the thought aside and replaced the photo. "You'd be proud of them all," he told her image. "You'd love their spouses, Isabella's most of all. Nick's an expert in medieval history, a man after your own heart."

He let his mind wander for a few minutes, remembering Aletta telling him at length about the museums she'd visited on her royal tour and how much she'd enjoyed the country's art. She'd hit Madrid's shops afterward, picking up fashions she hadn't seen in San Rimini. At the memory of her showing him a pink dress she thought would suit her complexion, he laughed aloud.

"You'd probably tell me to color my hair if you were here. You wouldn't like the gray at all. You'd say it made you look like you were married to an old man."

Though these days, despite the confidence he knew age and experience gave him, he felt younger than ever. Now that his children were happily married and he'd recovered from heart surgery, he had more energy and looked better than he had in years. He'd heard his staff comment on it when they thought he wasn't listening, and he'd read as much in the tabloids when he knew no one was looking over his shoulder at his reading material.

And for the first time in years, he'd looked twice at another woman. Why Claire Peyton, and why now, he couldn't guess. Maybe it was her backbone. Or the way she told a story. When she'd mentioned the scene in *Out of Africa* and the history of the ambassador's house, he'd been riveted. Though others might've found the topics boring, she'd seemed to sense his interest. Then again, perhaps there was nothing to it. Just his mind playing tricks, given the anniversary of

Aletta's death and his annual visit to the royal family's crypt at the Duomo.

He'd come to dread visiting Aletta the last three or four years. Not because of her, but because the entire day felt staged. The media stationed themselves across the street, their array of cameras aimed at the Duomo steps with the goal of capturing a momentary look of anguish to show the world that the king still mourned his beautiful queen. But Eduardo no longer felt the anguish when he thought of her, only a dull, leaden ache. And that, only when he shared a moment of joy with one of his children—such as at the birth of a grandchild—and regretted that Aletta wasn't able to experience it herself.

Somehow, over the years, Aletta had transformed in his mind almost as much as she had in the mind of the public. She'd become an image to rally around, someone to hold out to the world as a symbol of the romance and beauty of San Rimini, just as the late Princess Grace had become a symbol of Monaco.

She'd become someone—something—different than the woman who'd entered his life so long ago.

The phone on his desk rang, startling him. He leaned forward and hit the speaker.

"Your Highness," Luisa's clear voice came across the line, "I'm sorry to interrupt you, but the florist would like to know if you have any particular arrangement in mind."

He frowned to himself. "Plain white roses, same as last year. Loose is fine. No need for a vase."

"Excuse me. I wasn't clear. I meant the arrangement for Ambassador Peyton."

He swiped a hand over his face. He never lost concentration like this, never dwelled on the personal side of his life. His country demanded his full attention and he liked it that way. "I'm sorry, Luisa. I should have specified. You can tell the florist to use whatever is in season. Something uplifting and local. We want the ambassador to feel welcome in San Rimini."

He heard a familiar voice in the background and paused. "Count Giovanni Sozzani, I presume?"

Luisa made a noise of affirmation. "He stopped to drop off—what is it?—oh, I see. He stopped to drop off a book he borrowed from you."

"He could have brought it Sunday."

Luisa repeated the statement, then Eduardo heard a male voice say, "I was in the building and had it with me. Why send flowers to the embassy, Your Highness? Did you insult the new ambassador already?"

His friend was teasing him for the amusement of the staff, Eduardo knew, but since the two of them weren't in the same room with the ability to make eye contact, Giovanni had no idea his comment hit the mark.

"Luisa, please tell the count to leave the diplomacy to me, then inform him that I look forward to beating him at cribbage this Sunday."

"Yes, Your Highness." She relayed the message, then heard Giovanni's robust laugh as he said goodbye to the staff. Luisa quickly came back on the line and said, "I'll ask the florist about her stock of local flowers. I believe he'll be able to deliver the arrangement this afternoon, as soon as the card is ready."

"I'm writing it now." Making the delivery today was good. The press would salivate if they spotted a florist making a delivery to the embassy on the same day he was at the Duomo. Whether or not the flowers were sent as an official courtesy, some news outlet would post a misleading headline speculating on whether the king had a new romantic interest.

The thought made him realize what he'd done. He pressed a hand to his forehead, astounded at the mistake he'd nearly made. "Luisa, could you check something? Do I have any dinners scheduled for Friday?"

"Not a dinner, but you have the Our Place reception that runs from six to eight p.m. After that, you have thirty minutes with Sergio to discuss the Strada il Teatro project, then three phone calls to congratulate the winners of the national library essay contest."

He remembered now. "All right. What about Saturday?"

1 2

1 2 4 1 2

1 2 41 2 4 1 21 2 4 1 2 4

"Saturday you have breakfast with Prince Marco in his palace apartment. After that, a few quick meetings, then a luncheon at the aquarium to celebrate their new conservation initiative. You're free in the evening."

"All right. If Samuel could make arrangements, let's move dinner with Ambassador Peyton from Thursday to Saturday. That way she has more notice." It would also give the dinner separation from his visit to the Duomo. Such separation shouldn't be necessary, but he wasn't willing to take a chance.

"I'll talk to Samuel, but I don't foresee a problem."

"Thank you, Luisa. I'll have the note to you shortly."

After hanging up, he pushed aside the briefing folder, opened his desk drawer, and located a monogrammed notecard. Though he sent several personal notes each week, he stared at the card for a moment, at a loss for words.

Dear Madam Ambassador was as far as he got when a child's happy yell echoed from outside.

Latching onto the excuse, he rose, left the study, and strode to the far side of the great room, where one of the windows afforded a view of the palace garden. Eduardo leaned out the open window just in time to see Prince Federico's two sons, Paolo and Arturo, racing toward the private lawn that was located on the far side of the rose garden. The boys enjoyed wrestling in the grass, kicking balls, and climbing trees in the open area whenever possible. Eduardo smiled to himself as the boys tore along the gravel path, then disappeared from view.

It didn't surprise him to see Federico start jogging to catch up with his sons, despite the fact he wore a business suit and dress shoes. This was an entirely different Federico than the dutiful, contemplative man he'd been for most of his life. After being suddenly widowed a few years ago, he'd struggled to find meaning in his royal role as he raised a pair of toddlers who were deep in mourning for their mother.

But the recent changes in Federico had been positive. He'd found the strength to move on and had fallen in love with a wonderful woman. Pia Renati made Federico livelier and happier than Eduardo ever would have imagined in the weeks and months following the loss of Lucrezia, the boys' mother. Though the prince worked as hard as ever and remained a rule-follower at heart, Pia had helped Federico find a lightness of being that softened the stress lines that had taken up residence around his eyes. The two of them even planned a hiking trip in Columbia next month...without the children, and without a single public outing or political meeting on their agenda. Federico never would have done such a thing before Pia came into his life.

Nor would he have smiled so broadly as he ran through the garden.

Eduardo closed the window and returned to his study. Perhaps it was time he moved on as well. Stop mentally living in the past, stop acting like the stoic widower, and start allowing himself to consider the possibilities—what would life be like if he let himself think outside the fishbowl existence of the royal palace?

He took a seat, squared the notecard in front of him, and—after yet another call to Luisa to update the order—he began to write.

CHAPTER 5

CLAIRE TURNED OFF THE FAUCET, dried her hands, then eyeballed the floor along the stalls to ensure she was alone in the restroom. Confident she finally had a moment of solitude, she braced her hands on either side of the sink and allowed her shoulders to sag.

She was nearly done for the day. At least, nearly done with embassy work. She'd had a total of seven meetings since breakfast, if one counted coffee and a slice of toast grabbed on the way out of the hotel as breakfast. There'd been a briefing on a joint project involving the United States Drug Enforcement Administration and San Rimini's drug enforcement agency, discussions regarding several exchange programs, progress reports on American businesses that had been coordinating with the embassy on trade opportunities, and even a meeting with the embassy's protocol officer, who was in charge of ensuring Claire's public events went off without a hitch.

All the while, Claire had been internally repeating the names of staff members to help commit them to memory.

Tonight, she planned to put on her softest pajamas, curl up on the loveseat in her hotel room, and treat herself to a bottle of premium San Riminian wine. Then, she would sleep like a rock. She needed to. Tomorrow she was scheduled for a long session with John

Oglethorpe, the Public Affairs Officer, for an introduction to the press office. After that, she would take possession of the ambassador's residence. Rich Cartwright's belongings had been packed and inspected and the moving crew would arrive at the crack of dawn to transport everything to California.

"Half an hour," she told herself. She should only need thirty minutes with Karen to ensure her notes from this morning's meetings were handled and the resulting tasks were logged in her calendar, then she could enjoy the wine and close her eyes.

The first weeks on a new job were always the hardest, she reminded herself. In this case, it was particularly challenging because the embassy maintained a sizable staff, nearly all of whom had come on board during Richard Cartwright's tenure. It was natural for them to be skeptical of change and watch her every move to see what tone she would set.

"It'll get easier," she murmured to the mirror. She ran a hand over her hair, double-checked her teeth and lipstick, then made her way to her office. As she reached the doorway, a young man stood outside talking to Karen, his face partially blocked by the large plant he carried. The florist's pail in which it grew had been printed with the colors of the San Riminian flag and was tied in a large white bow.

Karen heard her coming and spun. "Madam Ambassador, you have a gift."

"I see." She thanked the man and urged him to carry the pail inside. She cleared a section of her desk and—since he could hardly see around the plant—guided him as he set it down.

Once he'd departed, Karen said, "Well, there must be a story to this."

"I can't imagine what." Claire leaned forward and looked at the leaves. "It's an olive."

"An olive? As in a tree?"

Claire glanced toward the hallway. There were several staff members within earshot, so she spoke in a voice modulated for Karen's ears alone. "You once told me I need a shovel to do my job.

Well, this time I really need a shovel." A little louder, for those in the hall, she said, "I need to find a spot to plant this."

"You do have a small yard at the residence."

"I suppose I do. It will make a nice addition." She circled the desk until she found the card. As she pulled it from the side of the florist's pail, she said, "Who sent it?"

"It came from the palace."

Karen's voice was all business, but her back was to the door and she gave Claire a wide-eyed look of fake innocence.

"What a kind welcome," Claire said, matching Karen's official tone. She opened the card, then started laughing. She couldn't help it.

"Madam Ambassador?"

Claire could hardly speak. She raised a hand until she finished reading. Once she gathered herself, she said, "It's from King Eduardo. He says this is a Banduzzi olive, which is native to San Rimini. While Banduzzi olives are prized for their oil, they're also served as table olives once cured."

"You're amused by a horticultural lesson?"

"Wildly," she said with a grin. "He also notes that an olive is a sign of peace and he would be honored if I would attend an informal dinner at the palace this Saturday. He promises to have Banduzzi olives available, should I wish to taste one. I am also invited to present my ideas on education or any other topics I might wish to discuss."

"You're joking."

"I am not. I assume I'm clear on Saturday for a meeting with King Eduardo?"

Karen blinked. "Yes, of course. I'm supposed to pick up the keys to my new flat and sign the paperwork at five. I'm sure I can move it—"

"That's all right. This looks like an invitation for one. Go get the keys to your flat."

Karen frowned. "Are you sure? I can call King Eduardo's office to clarify."

"I'll be fine."

Karen hesitated a beat, then said, "You haven't had the opportunity to meet him yet, but Mark Rosenburg manages the embassy's education and culture programs. He's in Atlanta touring Emory University and the Centers for Disease Control with a group of San Rimini's public health students and won't return until Monday. If King Eduardo agrees to support your program, Mark will be involved. I can't imagine the king didn't mean to include him."

"I'll contact him tonight to let him know about the invitation. Regardless of whether he was meant to be included, given the attitude of the king's chief political advisor, we should strike while the iron's hot. I'll personally give Mark a full briefing when he returns, then loop him in on future meetings."

At Karen's nod, Claire continued, "Speaking of meetings, I want to go through today's notes and update the calendar."

For the next twenty minutes, they ran through summaries of the meetings Claire had attended over the course of the day, then discussed her upcoming schedule. As they spoke, the employees in the hallway gradually withdrew. Lights over desks were extinguished and computers shut down for the evening. Finally, Claire set aside her notepad and took a long drink of water. Her brain was fried. "Tell me we're finished."

"We are."

"Thank goodness. Get a good night's sleep, Karen. Tomorrow is another day."

"Yes, and it'll be a long one."

Claire smiled as they both stood. "So you found a flat?"

"I did. No balcony and only this much sea view." Karen held her hands shoulder width apart, palms facing each other. "But it's only a fifteen-minute walk from here and the kitchen is glorious. San Rimini's produce markets are supposed to be amazing. I plan to do a lot of cooking."

"Funny, I plan to do a lot of eating."

Karen's smile widened for a moment, then her gaze went to the olive and she grew serious. No one was in earshot, but she lowered her voice anyway. "Ma'am, that was a handwritten card. From the king himself. It's my understanding that he doesn't do that often. I mean, he does for personal notes, but not for something like this, not anything official."

"What are you saying?"

Karen hesitated.

"You can be frank, Karen. We're alone."

They'd worked together for years and Claire considered Karen a friend. Still, it took Karen several seconds to answer. "He wouldn't have sent that card to Rich Cartwright."

"We don't know that." She didn't even need to gauge Karen's reaction before she relented. "All right, we know that."

"That dance was also out of character. It may have meant more than you think. Or more than you are willing to admit."

"Well, I did ask you to be frank."

"I'm sorry, Madam Ambassador—"

"No, don't be." She sighed. "I asked for your opinion because I value it, but I don't think the handwritten note is because of the dance. I suspect it's a San Riminian thing. Women are treated as equals here in regard to pay and opportunity, but the country still holds to Old World tradition when it comes to social niceties. Gifts and small kindnesses are considered the norm. Men still feel they should open doors for women. They take the outside position when walking on a sidewalk with a woman and at meals they wait for a woman to drink first."

Karen glanced at the olive tree. "Sounds like you paid close attention during the protocol meeting today."

"That I did." She began to gather her belongings. "Let's take this at face value. Send a response to the palace letting the king know that I'd be pleased to attend dinner on Saturday. Between now and then, I'll work on a pitch. We know from Sergio Ribisi that the king is reluctant to back the project. What we don't know is why. Let's brainstorm different approaches. Look into educational programs he's backed in the past and see where we can find commonalities. I'll ask Mark Rosenburg for his thoughts when I talk to him."

"Perfect."

"Oh, and we need to find out if there's a particular brand or type of alcohol the king prefers."

Karen paused. "Getting him drunk is not an approach I'd recommend."

"As a gift. Not a strategy."

"I'll have a bottle of something for you to present as a gift. I'll find something traditionally American to accompany it."

"Great." Claire stopped. "On second thought, find out what he likes, then let me know. I might have an idea."

"Will do."

She followed Karen out of her office, then headed for the embassy exit. Over her shoulder, she said, "I mean it, Karen. Get some sleep."

After she had a glass of wine and a few hours of lazing about in her pajamas, Claire promised herself she'd sleep, too. She'd earned it.

THERE WAS something about hearing the sound of his own footsteps on centuries-old stone that brought Eduardo peace.

By the time he reached the family crypt, his annoyance at the spectacle outside the Duomo walls had abated. The massive cathedral was as always: glorious, cavernous, and cool. It was also quiet, save for the muted sound of tourists whispering on the opposite side of the nave, where they'd gathered to enter a small chapel that contained paintings by Tintoretto and Raphael. Though the Duomo staff offered to close the building for an hour each year so Eduardo could make his visit in peace, he refused. Only the area surrounding the diTalora crypt would be roped off, and then only for as long as was required to complete his visit.

His chief of security, Chiara Ascardi, had once again told him that it would be easier to close the entire building.

"Next year, for the tenth," he'd promised her. "The media will make it impossible for the tourists and worshippers to visit then, no matter what we do. But for now, I'd prefer to keep it open. Who knows if this is a tourist's only chance to see the cathedral? I don't want anyone who has plans to see the building to miss it."

Now Chiara stood about twenty paces away, her back to him and her eyes sweeping the area to ensure no one approached. Other members of his security team blended into the background, acting as tourists or Duomo staff.

Eduardo lifted his chin and took in the sight of the stunning stained glass window over the crypt. "You would have loved the restoration work," he whispered to Aletta. "The craftsmen hired for the project did an amazing job."

Raising money to clean and restore the Duomo's windows, which had deteriorated thanks to centuries of grime, had been one of Aletta's pet projects. Roughly half the required funds had been raised at the time of her death. In her honor, King Carlo and Queen Fabrizia of Sarcaccia had donated the remainder of the amount from their private holdings.

It was a gift he thought of each time he entered the sacred space. Aletta had been loved by millions of people who didn't know her personally. But she'd been deeply loved by those who did, including Carlo and Fabrizia. Fabrizia, in particular, had become a mentor of sorts to Aletta after he and Aletta had become engaged, offering guidance on the challenges of living life in the public eye.

Eduardo smiled at the memory of Fabrizia and Aletta sitting together at the San Rimini Grand Prix. While he and Carlo had watched the drivers pick up speed along the straightaway where the royal box was located, the two queens sat with their heads together, trying to hold a conversation in spite of the noise from the engines and the crowd. It was shortly after Aletta had given birth to Antony, their eldest child, and it was the first time she'd left him to attend a public event.

Fabrizia had been the perfect person to accompany his wife that day.

Eduardo tore his gaze from the windows, then knelt to lay the white roses he carried atop the stone that honored his wife.

Ten minutes later, he stood just inside the cathedral's massive front doors, waiting for Chiara's signal that his car was waiting outside and all was secure. At her nod, he exited to a cacophony of cameras and reporters. He maintained a sober expression, as was befitting the occasion, and mentally tamped down his irritation at having to speak.

Ignoring the shouted questions, he said, "Thank you for coming. Queen Aletta would have been deeply touched by the love that the citizens of San Rimini—the citizens of the whole world—still hold for her in their hearts."

He paused, waiting for the media to quiet, then continued, "Queen Aletta is deeply missed by her friends and family because she made the world a better place. Today, rather than mourn her death, she would have preferred we honor her legacy by taking a moment to do as she would do. To that end, this morning I visited one of her favorite places, the Royal Memorial Hospital, and spent time speaking with both staff and patients. I also made donations on behalf of the royal family to several of her favorite charities so their positive work may continue. I urge those of you who wish to honor her to do the same. Donate your time, your money, or your voice to these great causes. Again, thank you. My family and I are appreciative."

Eduardo's feet moved the instant the final word left his lips. He was in the car and away from the Duomo less than a minute later.

Oh, Aletta, he thought. *Next time I visit, I'll do it without the cameras. And I promise that it'll be more meaningful.*

CHAPTER 6

It looked like a date.

Eduardo tried to ignore the subtle glances of Samuel Barden's staff as they busied themselves readying his apartment for the ambassador's arrival. Though Luisa had informed him that multiple palace venues were available tonight, he'd decided to stick to his original plan and host the dinner for Claire Peyton in his residence. Wind could be a factor if they dined on the rear patio, the family dining room was subject to interruptions on the weekend, and even Sergio agreed that the state dining room was too formal for a one-on-one dinner.

He'd hosted numerous small dinners here before. When guests were expected, certain staff members had permission to move in and out with little more than a cursory knock, which made the residence feel more public than private. This evening's setup felt different, however, and even the staff seemed attuned to it. He couldn't put a finger on the reason. Perhaps the selection of linens and floral arrangements brightened the room more than usual.

He took a seat and typed a few notes into his phone in order to tune out the goings on around him.

"Your Highness?"

Luisa's approach startled him, even though she'd called less than five minutes earlier to ask if she could stop by the residence. He gestured for her to take a seat in the chair adjacent to the sofa and accepted the sheaf of papers she offered him. "Coverage of last night's speech for Our Place?"

"Yes, sir." She waited as he flipped through the pages. When he neared the end, she said, "It seems to have gone well. There was a lot of positive press for the program's five-year anniversary."

"Well, it's about time they got off the Queen Aletta anniversary."

He heard how it sounded the instant the words left his mouth and was horrified. He blew out a hard breath. "I'm sorry, Luisa. I never should have said that. It doesn't in any way reflect my feelings."

"It does, but not your feelings about the queen," she said softly, offering him an understanding smile. "The media has been relentless all week. You've been incredibly patient and circumspect."

"Thank you. I appreciate that." He angled his head and studied her. "Don't take this the wrong way, but why are you at the palace today? Shouldn't you be enjoying your weekend?" He raised the papers she'd just handed him. "This could have waited until Monday."

"I had correspondence to catch up on and nothing going on at home, so I decided to come in. Margaret Halaby also happened to be in the office and left the media summary on my desk. When I saw how much good press the event received, I knew you'd want to see it."

"And you wanted to see the residence."

She started to deny it, but her eyes drifted to the far side of the room, where the staff continued to fuss over the table arrangements.

"It looks too romantic." It was a statement, not a question, but a rare grimace registered on Luisa's face.

"Your Highness, if you'll forgive me for saying so, well—"

"No, no. You don't have to say it aloud. Your expression makes your thoughts clear enough. I'll have them change it. I don't know what Samuel thought I had in mind when I said I'd invited the new U.S. Ambassador to dinner, but this seems more flowery than usual."

"The flowers themselves are fine, but perhaps you could ask Samuel's staff to remove the candles and raise the overhead lighting."

She paused, then added, "If you still think the pink flowers are too much, they could be switched with the arrangement that's on the hall table outside Prince Antony's apartment. It would work with the linens, but it's smaller and white."

"I'll do that." He aimed a look at the handbag tucked against Luisa's hip. "You're heading home?"

"Yes, though I did want to hear about today's luncheon at the aquarium. And your breakfast with Prince Marco."

"Breakfast was postponed to tomorrow. Amanda wasn't feeling well. But the aquarium was wonderful. Have you visited recently?" When Luisa shook her head, he described the newest exhibits and suggested she take her teenage nephew sometime soon. "They're showing a new documentary on marine conservation he'd love. It's fascinating. I wish I'd been able to stay for the entire film."

"He's spending a weekend with me next month while my sister and her husband attend a wedding in Switzerland. I'll reserve tickets and we can make a day of it." They chatted for another minute, then she wished him a good night and said she'd see him on Monday.

"Enjoy the rest of your weekend, Luisa. Thank you for the report and the dinner assistance."

He walked her to the door, then used the dimmer switch to adjust the lights in the great room to a level more appropriate for a business meeting. He dropped the papers on the desk in his study, then introduced himself to Emilia, the young woman who was arranging the flatware. He complimented her on the overall presentation, but asked her to remove the candles and switch the centerpiece for the one Luisa had suggested. Satisfied the romantic decor would be toned down, he headed to his bedroom suite to freshen up.

It was odd. Samuel had planned dozens of table arrangements for dinners over the past few years, but none had looked like that. And he couldn't remember the last time Luisa had come to the office on a weekend. He might work seven days a week, but he refused to burn out his staff members by requiring them to do the same.

Which made him wonder: why had Margaret Halaby stopped by his office to deliver the media report on his Our Place appearance?

Typically such material would be covered in their regular Monday morning meeting.

He studied himself in the mirror as he brushed his teeth. Did the whole palace think he was undergoing a midlife crisis? Because he'd danced with an ambassador and invited her to dinner?

He spit into the sink, then rinsed.

No, he decided, his imagination was getting the better of him. Samuel mentioned there had been turnover in the kitchen recently due to the retirement of several longtime employees. If the staff members setting up the table were sneaking looks at him, or were arranging the table in a different way, that was the most likely explanation. They were getting used to their new roles.

This time of year was beginning to make him paranoid. The news media wasn't alone in sensationalizing his relationship with Aletta. Souvenirs with their wedding photos were sold in every tourist shop in the country. Restaurants posted photos of her visits in their windows and on their websites. Even a local beach that had served as the site of their first date—a group outing with friends when he and Aletta were teenagers—often touted that fact to draw visitors.

Then there were the stories. A fictionalized version of his and Aletta's relationship had appeared on television in the United Kingdom and two miniseries had aired in the United States within two years of Aletta's death. One of the American miniseries had been picked up by several European outlets and was broadcast at this time each year.

Apparently another television movie on Aletta's life was in production in Egypt, though he had only heard about that one through word of mouth. He'd been told the producers planned for it to be aired on the tenth anniversary of her death.

Ridiculous as it sometimes felt, the world's obsession with Aletta Masciaretti wouldn't change. He needed to trust that his staff knew him better than the media did. He wasn't on a date, nor should he have concerns that was what they believed.

Besides, he barely knew Claire Peyton. She was intelligent, of course—she needed to be in order to do her job—and she was both attractive and single. But he knew dozens, probably hundreds, of women near his age who fit that description. And never once had a member of his staff expressed concern that he'd buy a red Ferrari and go zipping along the coast with a different woman in the passenger seat every weekend.

He checked his hair and teeth a final time, then exited the bathroom. He was *not* having a midlife crisis.

He finished his preparations and strode into the great room just as Miroslav Vulin, a massive Serbian man who worked closely with Chiara Ascardi in palace security, knocked and entered. "Your Highness, Ambassador Peyton's car just entered the rear gate. If you're ready, I'll escort her here."

"Thank you, Miroslav."

Not long afterward, Eduardo heard the click of the vestibule door being opened, then the tap of heels on the hardwood and the heavier tread of Miroslav's feet.

Miroslav entered, then gestured for Claire to move into the great room. "Your Highness, Ambassador Peyton is here for dinner."

He crossed the room as Claire entered. To Miroslav, he said, "Thank you." To Claire…well, to Claire he said, "Welcome," though he was suddenly at a loss for words.

She thanked Miroslav for the escort as he departed, then turned from the door and shot him a smile he felt clear to his bones.

If anyone had the potential to send him along the road to a midlife crisis, he decided right then and there it would be Claire Peyton. She looked stunning. He shouldn't notice that about an ambassador, but he did. Her eyes were warm and lively, her lips curved into a soft pink smile, and though her cream-colored suit and light blue blouse were perfectly suited to business, they also perfectly suited her figure.

He hadn't been this disconcerted about being alone with a woman since his first solo date with Aletta and he'd been sixteen at the time.

"The residence is lovely," she said as she moved forward and shook his hand. "I appreciate the invitation to dinner here."

He thanked her and, grateful for the opportunity to latch onto a subject that would help clear his thoughts, he added, "The room was recently refurbished. It hadn't been updated since well before my father was born. Every wall was covered in heavy brocade wallpaper. Having it removed made quite a difference."

She took a long look around the room, which was now covered in a pearl white paint. The baseboards had been stripped of years of wax, then refinished in their original dark color. The contrast gave the room a luminescent quality, especially at this time of day, as the sun set.

"It must have been quite dark in here, given that there are so few windows," she said. "I'm surprised an update wasn't completed earlier. You strike me as the type who prefers to surround yourself with all things light and bright rather than cocoon yourself in a dark room."

He smiled at that. Most people who visited the residence commented on the color, rather than the feeling it evoked. "I try not to hide away anywhere."

"Surely even a king needs respite from the world now and then."

"Now and then, but I don't consider respite the same as hiding." He cocked his head. "As an ambassador, you're often the center of attention. When you need time to yourself, do you consider it hiding?"

"I don't, but when my phone is turned off, my staff does."

"How often do you turn your phone off?"

She laughed and he loved the sound of it. "Almost never."

"So you don't hide, either." He gestured toward the bar, which was discreetly tucked against the wall near the entrance to his study. "May I offer you a drink before dinner?"

"I would love one, thank you." She glanced around as he crossed the room and opened the cabinet doors. "You're pouring?"

"Contrary to what most people believe about royalty, we're entirely capable of preparing our own drinks. Or drinks for guests." He scanned the bottles, then said, "I believe the chef plans to serve red wine with dinner, but I have the ingredients for a Negroni or an Aperol spritz, and the staff had the forethought to leave fresh ice. I also make a decent Manhattan. What would you like?"

"What are you having?"

"When I drink these days, it's usually whiskey. But in the spirit of going light and bright rather than dark, I'll have a Negroni."

"Then make it two."

As he opened the gin and measured it into a cocktail shaker, Claire asked, "You said 'when you drink these days.' Meaning?"

He capped the gin bottle, then tapped his chest with two fingers. "I had heart surgery a few years ago to repair a defect. All is well, but I err on the side of caution."

"I remember reading about that. I'm glad to hear that you're healthy."

He aimed a wry look at her as he added Campari to the shaker. "You weren't briefed?"

"I was, but I was also given background on a slew of parliament members, your chief justice, and several other prominent citizens. That much information at once tends to run together in a person's head."

Once he had all the ingredients, he put the lid on the shaker and gave it several flicks of the wrist, studying Claire's face as he did so.

"I don't think much runs together in your head. I suspect when it comes to your job, you keep everything straight."

"What makes you say that?"

He poured, then handed Claire her tumbler. "The President wouldn't have assigned you to San Rimini if you weren't intelligent. You also have backbone. Most in your position would have kept silent if Sergio warned them not to raise a topic with me. You called me out on his warning, but you did it with grace."

"Was it grace that earned me tonight's invitation? Or guilt?"

His eyes caught hers. Energy sizzled between them, so strong it was almost palpable. Neither of them looked away. They'd each been too well trained for their jobs to ever look away. But in this case, the underlying tension had nothing to do with work.

It took Eduardo a few beats to answer. "The invitation was sent because you deserve to be heard. Over Sergio's objections, I might add."

"It's his job to watch your political back."

"Yes."

"He does it well. Your approval rating is very high."

"I like to believe that's due to my irresistible personality and sparkling wit rather than Sergio's political acumen, but let's not tell Sergio."

"I have no intention of doing so." She took a sip of her Negroni and her brows lifted in approval. "You really do know how to mix a drink, Your Highness."

"If I'm ever forced to abdicate, I'll keep bartending in mind as a backup."

That made her grin. "Well, on that note, it's my understanding that one never attends a dinner in San Rimini empty-handed."

She moved toward the vestibule, where he spotted a bag he hadn't noticed before. She must have set it down as Miroslav escorted her inside. She bent to catch the handles, then returned and presented it to him. He gave her a questioning look before he reached inside and partially withdrew a large bottle of whiskey.

"Colkegan Single Malt," he read aloud.

"Product of New Mexico. Don't forget that part. It's my home state."

"I had no idea that New Mexico produces whiskey."

"There are a few boutique distilleries. I thought you'd enjoy trying an American whiskey."

"I will. Thank you."

He slipped the bottle back inside the bag and was about to place it on top of the bar when she said, "There's more."

Curious, he took a second look inside the bag. Sure enough, there was a small glass container at the bottom. When he read the label aloud, he couldn't disguise his amusement. "Prickly Pear jelly?"

"Made with green chiles from New Mexico. It's good stuff, but I offer no guarantees as to whether it's easier on the heart than whiskey."

"Are you hoping I drop dead? I must warn you that if you harm the monarch, diplomatic immunity won't cover you."

"Not at all. In fact, it would be rather inconvenient if you were to drop dead, given that you invited me here to discuss San Rimini's participation in a program that is near and dear to my heart. Consider it a peace offering."

He looked at the label again. "Prickly pear? And after I sent you an olive tree. One strikes me as more peaceful than the other. In fact, I was going to send flowers, something local to welcome you to San Rimini. But then I thought, 'what's more local than a Banduzzi olive?'"

"It's a lovely olive tree," she admitted. "You need to focus on the pear rather than the prickly."

"A peaceful prickly pear?"

"Bit of a tongue twister, isn't it?"

He laughed as he placed the gift bag on top of the bar. "How about this: I'll consider the whiskey a peace offering. It's good for mellowing the soul."

"On that point, we agree, Your Highness."

A knock sounded at the door. Eduardo told Claire, "I believe our dinner is here," then called out, "Please come in."

Emilia entered with a rolling cart. Samuel Barden trailed a few steps behind.

Eduardo looked at him in surprise. "Samuel, I didn't know you'd be here."

"Your Highness," the chef said with a slight dip of his head. "I wanted to ensure all was in order. I hope you're having a good evening?"

"I am, thank you. Madam Ambassador, may I present Samuel Barden. He is my personal chef and plans the menu whenever I host dinners such as this. And he is supposed to have today off."

"It's an honor, Madam Ambassador," he said, shaking Claire's hand.

"The honor is mine. Whatever you brought on that cart smells divine."

"Thank you, Ma'am. If anything is not to your liking, please let me know. It's my job to ensure that everyone who enters the king's residence leaves well fed."

"I'm certain I will."

Eduardo escorted Claire to the table and introduced Emilia, then

Samuel presented a pinot noir while Emilia filled their water goblets and set dinner before each of them.

Once all was in order, Eduardo thanked Samuel and Emilia, then assured them that all was well and that he would call when he and Claire were ready for dessert.

After they departed, Claire said, "He's worked for you for some time."

"He has. Before he became my personal chef, he ran catering operations for the entire palace. You should have seen the reception he managed when the King and Queen of Spain came for a state visit. There were over four hundred guests, yet each meal looked and tasted as if it had been cooked by a master chef for a private table."

The conversation turned to business topics after that. He told her about a threatened fisherman's strike his office had been monitoring and she shared news on an initiative a prominent American tech company hoped to pursue in San Rimini. That evolved into a debate on how the United States' latest trade agreement with the European Union would affect countries around the Adriatic, and he found himself settling into the usual cadence of all his business meetings.

Yet for the seriousness of the topics, the evening didn't feel like work. There was a lightness to their conversation that put him at ease. Good food and good wine helped, as did the setting.

"So, King Eduardo," Claire said, eyeing what was left of her salad and the elaborately garnished manicotti Samuel had served, "I sincerely hope this is your favorite meal."

He grinned at the light teasing in her tone. "And why is that?"

"Because you invited me here to discuss the education program and I'm about to do just that. I want you in a good mood."

He made a point of using his fork to expose the copious amounts of spinach inside his serving of manicotti. "I would prefer a good American cheeseburger with fries, but since my chef fears such a meal would put me into cardiac arrest, this is as good as it gets."

He meant it, too. Though Samuel did his best to create delicious meals, Eduardo couldn't remember the last time he had a meal containing anything close to the medical community's recommended daily limits of fat or sodium. He told Claire, "My staff doesn't seem to understand that cholesterol wasn't the problem. It was structural."

"They care about you."

"That they do and I'm grateful, which is why I eat what Samuel prepares, even when it involves flaxseed or mounds of vegetables. I also see a trainer three times a week who happens to be the first cousin of my personal assistant, Luisa. It keeps everyone happy."

"Everyone but you?"

"If they're happy, my life is considerably easier. It's worth it."

Claire tilted her head, making a show of studying his navy suit. "You're overdressed for a Big Mac. But I'll express your appreciation of our beef industry to the President and I'll see what I can do should you attend a dinner at the embassy."

"Even though you're a vegetarian? You represent your country and its interests well. I must keep that in mind."

Her soft brown eyes widened in surprise. "How did you know that?"

"It was a guess. I noticed that you ate the salad and the rice at the credentials ceremony, but didn't touch your cordon bleu. Apparently my staff hadn't been informed."

"That was entirely my fault. I was focused on the speech and the proper etiquette for the occasion and failed to communicate my dietary preferences. But I'll keep in mind that you watch what a woman eats."

"Only when I'm trying to assess her likes and dislikes," he admitted. "I've been trained from the day I was born to be polite, you know."

He took a sip of his wine, then set the glass near the tip of his knife. "For instance, Madam Ambassador, you're wearing a lovely outfit tonight."

A warm smile spread across her face, making it clear she enjoyed their banter. The lightness of her expression made his stomach clench, and he was old enough and wise enough to know exactly what that sensation meant.

He was developing a full-fledged crush on an ambassador.

CHAPTER 7

CLAIRE TRIED to ignore the bubble of attraction that fluttered through her.

She had wondered if the king was flirting with her when they'd danced at her credentials ceremony. The wink he'd given her was devastating.

But the look he gave her now was something else. She hadn't been on a date in a long while, but this felt like one, despite the topics of conversation.

She leaned back in her chair. "Are you hoping to distract me from discussing the education program, Your Highness? I'll remind you that you specifically mentioned it in your invitation."

"I did, and I wish to give it my undivided attention. How about this: I'll ring Samuel and ask for dessert, then we can discuss your ideas over sweets."

"I can agree to that."

He excused himself, picked up a phone located near his study, then spoke quietly for a few seconds before returning to the table. Within minutes, Samuel entered with Emilia. They asked about the meal, cleared the dishes, and offered coffee, tea, and a selection of cordials. Claire opted for decaffeinated coffee, saying that the Negroni and a glass of wine were as much alcohol as she ever consumed in one night. King Eduardo asked for tea.

As Emilia prepared their drinks, Samuel placed desserts in front of each of them. "I hope you like chocolate, Madam Ambassador?"

"I do," she assured him as she admired her plate, which contained a dome-shaped dark chocolate cake surrounded by an arrangement of berries and a sprig of fresh peppermint.

"I grow the peppermint myself and the berries are local, picked just yesterday," he told her. To the king, he said, "When you're ready, please call and Emilia will clear the dishes. I'll leave more tea and coffee on the bar."

The king thanked both Samuel and Emilia, then waited for them to depart before dropping a sugar cube into his tea.

"He gave me more berries and less cake than he gave you," Eduardo grumbled.

Claire looked across the table. It was true. Her cake wasn't large, but it visibly larger than the king's. "He wanted to ensure you get your antioxidants."

"That's an optimistic way of looking at it, though I should point out that chocolate is also an antioxidant."

"Dark chocolate is. I don't think the cake qualifies." At his look of consternation, she added, "I'll tell you what. Agree to support my education plan in parliament and I'll give you my dessert. All of it."

"I don't want the berries."

"Then the cake without the berries."

He laughed. It was a hearty, masculine laugh that made her toes curl inside her shoes. The kind of laugh that shouldn't affect her—particularly when she'd spent the past few days honing her pitch for the education program—but it did.

"Keep your cake," he said. "I can raid the kitchen after Samuel goes home if I need a chocolate fix. But do tell me about your plan."

She lifted her fork but hesitated before slicing into the cake. "First, why don't you tell me why Sergio Ribisi wanted to reject it before I could even present it."

"It wasn't Sergio. Not unilaterally. That was my call."

She snagged his gaze, surprised at the admission. "I appreciate the honesty, Your Highness."

"Even so, it should have been handled better."

"Why did it need to be 'handled' at all?"

Eduardo's jaw tightened for a moment, then he shrugged. "As king, I need to pick and choose my battles. There are days I would like to be an absolute monarch and pass laws I know to be in the best interest of the country, but we aren't living in the middle ages. I can introduce or recommend legislation, but that's as far as it goes. Parliament holds the power in San Rimini. And unlike your president, I don't have a veto."

"But you do have sway. A lot of it."

"Yes, but again, it's because I've chosen my battles carefully, as have my predecessors. Traditionally, in San Rimini, the monarch focuses on non-controversial projects. Most revolve around charitable initiatives, or serving as a mediator for peace talks or as a host for international summits. I have a limited amount of political capital to spend outside those parameters, so I have to spend it wisely."

"I understand that, King Eduardo. But if you've read about the program I worked to establish in Uganda, then you know it's for the public good. It's easy for people to think of the world as hundreds of disparate economies, but more and more, we have a single world economy. When one country—or one region—falls behind, it affects the others. Education is the great equalizer, particularly early education. When wealthier countries with strong educational systems contribute teachers and educational funding to the countries that struggle, everyone benefits, wouldn't you agree?"

"I do."

"Then why the resistance? Italy and Austria already participate, and I know you value early intervention programs to ensure children aren't deprived of educational opportunities. It's why you support programs like Our Place. When you spoke at their anniversary celebration yesterday, it wasn't out of obligation. It was plain to see that you're passionate about their work."

He had a forkful of cake halfway to his mouth and paused. "You saw it?"

"I did."

"You were doing research on me."

"I wouldn't be a good ambassador if I didn't."

She couldn't help but smile as she said it. When she'd called Mark Rosenburg, the embassy's education and cultural exchange specialist, to tell him about the dinner invitation from King Eduardo, he'd urged her to find a newsfeed showing the king's appearance at the event. Mark said she could learn a lot about King Eduardo's beliefs regarding education by listening to his speech and then use that information that to hone her pitch.

Mark had been right. When Eduardo spoke about the importance of Our Place, its success in identifying children who were struggling with mental health issues, and the methods used so their challenges were addressed without stigmatizing them, she saw his belief in the program.

Eduardo swallowed his bite of cake, then set down his fork. "The night you were here to present your credentials, there was a car accident on the Strada il Teatro. You likely saw it on the news."

"I did," she said, though she wasn't sure what it had to do with either Our Place or her education program.

"The accident could have been much worse. The Strada is the heart of our historical area. Every tourist who comes to San Rimini visits that street. Locals go for the ability to people watch or when they wish to dine at any of the dozens of restaurants in the area. It also has nonstop traffic and there's little to no parking. That's a bad combination."

He paused, as if wanting to ensure he had her attention. On a deep breath, he said, "Every resident of San Rimini is aware of the problem and knows it needs to change or there will be a tragedy. However, the appearance of the Strada is part of our national identity, which makes change difficult. Then there are the usual challenges of construction in a downtown area. Businesses don't want scaffolding blocking their entrances, hotels and restaurants are afraid they'll lose bookings due to either noise or diverted traffic, and the Grand Prix organizers have concerns about construction interfering with the course and viewing areas. Those are significant hurdles. No parliamentarian wants to be the one who sticks out their neck to make those improvements. Upset any one of those groups, and they're likely to be out of a job the next time voters go to the polls."

Claire studied the king. This wasn't simply an important issue to Eduardo; it was one he felt rested on his shoulders and his alone. "You're taking it on."

"Yes. No one can vote me out of office. On the other hand, this isn't an area in which monarchs traditionally get involved. I need every bit of the good will I've built during my years on the throne to get these groups unified behind a plan that will work. My popularity has never been as high as it is right now. Personally, I don't care about being liked. I'm old enough and have lived in the public eye long enough that I don't derive my self worth from what others think of me. But if my current popularity can be used to save lives—and I'm convinced that fixing the Strada il Teatro will save lives—then I need to pursue that opportunity. I can't spend my political capital to push parliament into sending funds or supporting teachers for an educational program in another country, particularly when San Rimini's citizens won't see the positive effects for years or decades."

Claire felt her body tensing as he spoke and forced herself to relax. There was conviction in his words, but she'd discovered over the years that convictions weren't always set in stone. Not when the person holding the conviction was reasonable, and was presented with good evidence that changing their stance could bring benefits.

She took a long sip of her coffee, considering her next words. Finally she asked, "You don't think it's possible to support both? They're completely separate issues. Given the success of Our Place, it would be easy for you to talk to your allies in parliament about the fact that instituting educational programs in poor, rural areas sets children on the right track."

He raised a hand. "I believe in what you've done in Uganda. You don't need to argue the point."

"You said it yourself the other night. You only gave it a quick read."

He surprised her by reaching across the table and covering her hand with his. "Not because it's not worthy of attention. Because it was obvious from the start that it's a worthy program and it has helped a lot of children. It will continue to help a lot of children and raise their standard of living. I didn't need to read every last detail to be convinced of that."

They both froze, as if simultaneously realizing the impropriety of the touch. At the same time, neither one of them wanted to acknowledge that impropriety by pulling away. After a long moment, Eduardo's grip tightened around her fingers, then he released her hand.

When he spoke again, there was gravel in his voice. "The program already has support from a number of governments. And with all due respect, you are no longer the ambassador to Uganda. The program is no longer yours."

"That's true," she said, relieved at the steadiness in her voice when she didn't feel steady at all. "However, the program was the signature piece of my tenure there and the current ambassador wants to expand the program. That means increasing the number of supporters. San Rimini has the ability to offer that support and it's natural that I'm the one to ask for it, both on behalf of the United States and my country's new ambassador in Uganda. Frankly, knowing I could do this when I came here made it easier for me to leave Uganda. A finishing touch, if you will. But if you don't support it to parliament, it will be difficult to pass."

He said nothing, but she could feel his resistance. She took a chance and fired her final shot. "If the program does not have the support of the government of the country to which I am now assigned, it doesn't look good for the program, Your Highness, and frankly, it does not look good for me. The President ran on a platform that focuses on education. It was the centerpiece of his inauguration speech. He spoke not only about the need for quality education for all Americans, but said that when children worldwide have access to education, their standard of living increases. They have better jobs.

Trade improves. Economies improve. There are fewer wars, and fewer refugees. Everyone wins."

"I believe that, as well." He straightened in his seat. "It's not that I can't offer any support. I can't offer any right now. Parliament meets in just under three months to consider the budget for improvements to the Central Business District. From now until then, the Strada must be my priority. Once it gets through, perhaps we can speak again."

Frustration welled up within her. She knew what 'perhaps' meant. It meant no. In a best-case scenario, King Eduardo would present his project to parliament with the agreement of all parties involved...and that would be tough to accomplish. It would be weeks, maybe months before parliament passed it—if they passed it—and months after that before construction began and who knew how long before it was complete.

He wouldn't want to use that time to advocate for another plan. Not while the country held its breath, waiting to see if the changes to the Strada would be positive. The king would be doing all he could to continue to support the Strada project until the last orange cone was removed from the construction area and the country deemed it worthwhile.

"The Strada project will take a great deal of time, should it pass."

"Yes. But the results will be long lasting. Well beyond my lifetime."

She nodded. "It's necessary. I haven't been in San Rimini long, but it only took one drive along the Strada to see the need. However, as you said, everyone in the country knows it needs to be done. Your citizens—and your parliament—will appreciate that you are the one putting your neck on the line, as you phrased it, in order to see it through."

"One can hope." There was caution in his voice. He'd been at the game long enough to know she was about to make another proposal.

"You know the members of parliament as well as anyone. If the Strada project were not at issue, which parliamentarians do you think would stand in the way?"

"Your staff has likely already told you."

They had. Mark Rosenburg, in particular, knew who had—and

who hadn't—been a supporter of similar initiatives. But to Eduardo, she said, "I'd like to get your perspective."

"Monica Barrata. Franco Galli. Luciano Festa. All three hold a great deal of sway. They usually raise objections over spending on foreign aid. They'd certainly raise objections over financing your program. Now, they'd say wonderful things about what has been accomplished in Uganda, but at the end of the day, they believe we need to focus on San Rimini first. They'll say that money should first go to our university programs, research programs, or infrastructure."

"All right."

He held up a hand. "They wouldn't be the toughest, however. That would be Sonia Selvaggi. She will have a number of objections. While she represents a single vote, she is a convincing speaker and will draw others to her side when it comes time to say yay or nay."

Mark had mentioned Selvaggi. Festa also sounded familiar.

Claire used her fork to swipe a berry along her plate so that it gathered the last of the cake crumbs on its surface, then popped it into her mouth. It was delicious and she envied Eduardo his chef. When she finished, she laid her fork across her plate. "What if I could convince those four?"

"I'd be impressed. It would be very difficult."

"Then I'd like to propose a deal. I get those four and you introduce my program to parliament."

"Introduce the program? That's quite a step up from simply speaking in support of it."

"You said those four would likely stand in the way and that they each hold a great deal of influence."

"Yes, but introducing the program would require more political capital than simply speaking in favor of it."

She smiled and spread her hands. "If I convince those four that the program is solid and worth being supported by parliament, the risks to you are much lower. You could afford to introduce it."

The king's blue eyes pierced her as he considered. As the seconds ticked by and he remained silent, Claire's heart thudded so hard she feared he could see her pulse at her throat. Only the thought that he hadn't rejected the idea outright kept her from saying, "never mind" or "all right, if I get those four, would you speak to others?"

With every hour she'd spent in San Rimini, she'd had more ideas of areas where the embassy could create positive changes. If she could get this program through, it would lend credence to every other initiative she and her staff pursued. The movers and shakers of San Rimini would see that she could not only fill Rich Cartwright's role, she could improve upon it.

"All right," Eduardo said. "You have a deal."

She could hardly believe it. She even heard the doubt in her tone as she repeated, "I get the support of those four parliamentarians and you'll introduce legislation to parliament to fund the education program and support sending teachers from San Rimini. That's the agreement?"

"Yes."

He stood and reached across the table. Claire couldn't get out of her seat fast enough. "Thank you, Your Highness."

His grin made her heart soar. Then there was his touch, the hand-shake held longer than necessary. Anyone watching them would have done so with wide eyes and a sharp intake of breath.

When he finally let go, Claire's insides did a hard flip.

She might have won the evening, but she was in deep, deep trouble.

CHAPTER 8

A BATTERED cribbage board rested between King Eduardo diTalora and Count Giovanni Sozzani. They sat at the same table where Eduardo had enjoyed dinner with Claire only twenty-four hours earlier. As Giovanni opened a deck of cards, Eduardo poured whiskey into a pair of crystal tumblers.

The cribbage board had once belonged to Giovanni's grandfather. When Eduardo and Giovanni were seventeen, Giovanni's grandfather was diagnosed with pancreatic cancer. The boys had gone to visit him at the hospital a few days before he entered hospice. Giovanni had indulged his grandfather's request to play a game of cribbage, though he had no idea what to do.

When Giovanni's grandfather passed away two weeks later, the cribbage board was on his bedside table along with a note: *Giovanni, this is yours. Play with your future king. Teach him something. Learn something from him.*

And so they did.

The boys found a book on cribbage, spent time learning the basics, and played a few games before abandoning it for more interesting pursuits. But one night, during their final year at university, Giovanni had appeared at Eduardo's door with the board tucked under one arm and a half-empty bottle of whiskey he'd nabbed from his parents' liquor cabinet the previous weekend in his other hand.

Giovanni's girlfriend of three years had left him for a Spaniard she'd met at a party the night before. Giovanni needed a mindless pursuit.

"Cribbage is not mindless," Eduardo had informed his friend.

Giovanni had raised the bottle. "It can be."

He'd stared at Giovanni. "She met him at a party?"

"After five minutes of conversation, she realized that he is the man for her and I am not. I suspect—though I did not confirm—that she took him back to her flat to validate this newfound knowledge."

Eduardo had grabbed the bottle of whiskey. "I'll make yours a double. We'll need a deck of cards."

"Have one in my back pocket."

The pair soon became addicted to what their friends considered a quaint hobby. At least once a month, usually on a Sunday, Eduardo and Giovanni met and played cribbage. All these years later, they used the same board, though a few of its pegs were discolored and the wood around nearly every hole showed scrapes. Before each game, they toasted Giovanni's grandfather.

Eduardo handed Giovanni a tumbler. They raised their glasses, then sipped. The liquid worked its magic on Eduardo in an instant. He relaxed into his chair, closed his eyes for a moment, and savored.

Sunday nights were his favorite. It was as if the entire country stilled for a weekly moment of reflection. Museums, shops, the aquarium, and most restaurants closed early. Tourists often used Sundays as a travel day, so the sidewalks stayed relatively uncrowded. Casino spotlights were prohibited from splitting the night sky and the predominant sounds were that of the sea breeze, the birds, and the occasional tolling of church bells.

The palace was also quiet, with all but essential staff at home. His children—and their children—usually spent the evening ensconced in their own palace apartments.

"What is this?" Giovanni asked as he tilted his glass to inspect his whiskey. "It's different than your usual."

"Is that good or bad?"

"Neither. It's different. Like eating rotini with pesto one day and puttanesca the next. This whiskey has more smoke to it. Where did you get it?"

"It was a gift."

They drew to determine who would deal first. Eduardo had the low card, a four of hearts to Giovanni's king of diamonds. He picked up the deck to shuffle as Giovanni reached for the whiskey bottle. "New Mexico? I've never heard of whiskey from New Mexico. That's the United States, not Mexico itself, correct?"

"Correct."

"Hmm." Giovanni spun the bottle in his hand, finished reading, then returned it to its previous spot. Though the sun had gone down, Eduardo had opened the curtain and cracked the window to let in the night air, so as he took another sip of his drink, Giovanni turned his face to the breeze and inhaled deeply.

"Whatever it is you are thinking, Giovanni, you're wrong."

"You sound like my wife."

"You aren't married."

Thirty years earlier, Giovanni *had* been married. But less than six months after the ceremony, his wife suddenly served him with divorce papers. As with Giovanni's university girlfriend, his wife had fallen for another man. Giovanni had an adult son from the relationship and loved being a parent, but he'd never remarried, despite the fact a number of women had pursued him over the years. Instead, he cracked jokes now and then about the wife he didn't have.

Giovanni sighed, then turned from the window to look at Eduardo. "So what is it you think I'm thinking?"

"You tell me."

Giovanni eyed him. "You receive a lot of gifts. It's impossible to keep or use them all."

Eduardo said nothing. He dealt the cards.

"I believe you asked Luisa to send flowers to the new United States ambassador when I stopped by your office earlier this week. Would that ambassador happen to be from New Mexico?"

"She would."

"And would this be the same ambassador with whom you shared a dance?"

"She was at the palace for the presentation of credentials. The ceremony was followed by a dinner with dancing. All of which I assume you know, if you're asking about the dance."

"What I know is that you rarely dance. Or send flowers to officials."

"I send flowers more often than you might believe. And whether I wish to or not, I'm occasionally compelled to dance at these events."

"Compelling is a good word for it."

Eduardo ignored the remark. After that, they concentrated on the game. Cards were laid on the table, points counted, and pegs moved along the board. Between hands, Giovanni shared news about his parents, whom he'd finally convinced to book a cruise along the coasts of Norway and Sweden. "They've been retired for nearly fifteen years now. They planned to spend their retirement traveling, yet they hardly leave their villa, let alone the country. It's one excuse after another. They need to take care of their dog. They need to be home for the electrician. They don't want to miss a local event, and there's always some local event. They finally realized that they aren't getting any younger and that they should go while they're still mobile enough to enjoy themselves."

Eduardo smiled. Giovanni loved to travel, while his parents had always been nervous about being away from the familiar. Still, he knew the cruise Giovanni had found for them would suit. They would appreciate the security of staying in the same cabin each night while having the opportunity to explore new places.

"I have news of my own," Eduardo told Giovanni. "I'm going to be a grandfather again. Marco and Amanda invited me to breakfast this morning and told me that Amanda is sixteen weeks pregnant. I suspected as much a few weeks ago, but wasn't going to ask. They wanted to wait as long as possible to announce the pregnancy."

"Sixteen weeks? That's quite far along. Surely some of the staff are already aware?"

"Apparently not. Marco said that Amanda has been engaged in 'creative dressing' for the past few weeks to hide it, but between staff interactions and Amanda's public schedule, it's becoming difficult. They had a doctor's appointment last week and said it was a challenge to get into the clinic unseen. They think they can pull off another week or two, but that's it. They plan to make a public announcement a week from this Wednesday." He smiled at his friend. "I'm going to have a granddaughter."

Giovanni raised his glass, and they toasted again.

Several hands later, when Giovanni collected the cards and started to shuffle, Eduardo took the opportunity to stand and stretch his legs. He reached for the whiskey and offered to refill his friend's drink.

"Only if you refill yours."

Eduardo sighed. "It'll have to be with water. Then I can answer honestly when Greta grills me about it tomorrow morning. She knows I have whiskey on cribbage nights."

Giovanni waved a hand. "Get your water. I'll pour my own whiskey."

When Eduardo returned from the bar, water in hand, Giovanni said, "If you're in the mood to answer honestly…?"

Eduardo raised a brow.

"You're distracted tonight. I'm the better player, obviously, but I'm not that much better."

"You're not the better player."

"Then explain your performance. This isn't about becoming a grandfather again."

Giovanni knew him too well. Sometimes it was maddening, but tonight, Eduardo needed a friend. "I am considering asking a woman for a date."

Giovanni's boisterous laugh filled the room. "Is that all?"

Eduardo flashed a look of disgust. "It's not that simple."

"It is that simple, even for a king. And it's about time." Giovanni held up a hand before Eduardo could react. "You know I loved Aletta, but you deserve to have a woman in your life. The public will understand. Eventually."

"This isn't about that. Well, it's sort of about that. I have other concerns."

"Aside from the public reaction? I doubt your children would object, not that their objections should stop you." Giovanni frowned. "Are you considering the idea of dating in general or is there a particular woman who interests you?"

"There is a particular woman."

Giovanni said nothing. Instead, he collected the cards, then passed the deck to Eduardo so he could deal.

Eduardo felt a prickle of irritation as he shuffled. "That's all. I want to ask a particular woman for a date, but doing so is complicated."

"How so? Do you need me to ask one of this woman's friends if she likes you first? Or slip her a note that says, 'Please check the box yes or no. Do you like Eduardo diTalora?' I realize that's how it was the last time you were interested in any female besides Aletta, but that's not how it's done these days. It's not complicated. You simply ask a woman if she'd like a date. Then she says yes or she says no."

"I shouldn't have suggested a second glass of whiskey."

"Of course you should have. I give my best advice after the second glass."

Eduardo shook his head, then tried to focus on the count. It didn't matter. Giovanni hit the target score almost immediately, ending play.

"I was thinking of asking her to the symphony," he said. "The season begins next week and I usually attend one of the early performances."

"You can't take a date there. *Think*, Eduardo."

He met Giovanni's gaze, then realization dawned. "It's the Queen Aletta Concert Hall."

"Given the range of salacious headlines the media could run, they'd be ecstatic. You and your date, not so much. This woman must be something else, because that is not a misstep the Eduardo I know is prone to make." Giovanni moved a peg to score his last play, then looked up sharply. "Wait. You're talking about the new ambassador?"

"Yes. Claire Peyton."

"I was teasing you about the flowers earlier. I had no idea."

Giovanni made a low noise of dissatisfaction. "I'm apparently the one who's distracted tonight, as I completely misread your reaction. She's quite attractive."

"Yes."

"She bewitched you with smoky whiskey."

Eduardo let the comment go. He wasn't about to tell Giovanni that the gift also included prickly pear jelly.

"Now I see why you say it's complicated, though the words I'd use are conflict of interest."

"If I were in parliament or if I were the head of any of a number of government departments, the conflict would be far worse."

"True, but that doesn't mean there isn't a conflict."

"It's one that can be avoided, with care." Eduardo studied his friend. "I like her, Giovanni."

"That much is apparent." Giovanni ran a finger along the base of his whiskey glass. "If she's smart, she'll say no."

"She *is* smart. She likes history and movies and she cares about the greater good. She's also not intimidated by me, by which I mean all of this." He swirled his hand to encompass the palace. "She isn't afraid to let me see her wit. That's why I like her."

"She's also hot."

"Fine. She's hot," he admitted. "If the symphony is out, what about the Royal Theater? The final performance of *La Traviata* is the annual fundraiser for the Royal Foundation of San Rimini. Isabella usually attends with me, but now that she's married, it wouldn't be surprising for me to take someone else. It's long been established that this is not a romantic night. Claire and I could make it a date without revealing that fact to the public."

"I doubt that telling your date that 'this is a date, but it's not a romantic night' is how a woman wants to be wooed."

"Because you know all about wooing women?"

Giovanni gave Eduardo a self-satisfied shrug.

"You're rich and handsome, Giovanni. That's not the same."

"If being rich were all it took to woo a woman, you'd be the king of us all."

"I *am* the king. And you forgot handsome."

"Oh, I didn't forget. Perhaps that's your problem. You aren't handsome enough. You'll have to rely on the wooing, which means doing it properly." His expression turned devilish. "By the way, how's it been going with Greta? How many pull-ups have you tallied in a row?"

"Go running with me sometime and I'll demonstrate when you finally make it to the finish line."

"Go biking with me sometime and you can demonstrate once you finish pushing your bike uphill."

"I have no desire to race a bicycle through city traffic. That's suicidal."

"We'll go early. About the same time you usually run."

Eduardo shook his head. Giovanni was a die-hard cyclist, always trying to recruit Eduardo to his sport of choice. "When my body won't tolerate running any more, I'll consider joining the dark side. It won't be anytime soon. Until then, you're welcome to join me on my run."

"If you need an exercise partner, I'd much rather join you for one of your sessions with Greta."

"She's married."

"Perhaps not, then."

The cards were dealt and more hands played. They counted aloud and moved pegs along the board. When Giovanni hit the target again and play ended, he turned serious. "Hypothetically, if you were to take Claire Peyton to the fundraiser at the Royal Theater, what would you hope to gain?"

Eduardo paused as he cleared the cards. "What do you mean, gain?"

"What is your end game? If you wish to date an ambassador—an ambassador from a powerful country that does a great deal of business in San Rimini—that must be considered. If you were to take Claire Peyton to the opera, it would be commented upon, both in the press and behind closed doors. By those in parliament. By your own staff. By every citizen sitting down to their evening meal. Even if it's presented to the world as a diplomatic outing, rather than a date, people will make assumptions. Some comments may not be kind. If you're going to take that risk, you need to know what it is you hope for. What's your end game?"

Eduardo shuffled slowly, then looked at Giovanni. "I felt a connection with her. I'm pretty sure she felt it, too. I want to spend time with her and get to know her. And I don't want to make up excuses to have her to the palace as a guest to do it. I want to take her out."

"Then you need to be prepared for the consequences, whether a relationship works out or not."

"I'm aware of that. I'm trying to anticipate what those consequences would be. I'm out of practice on this front."

"Successful relationship or not, your popularity will suffer a blow."

He'd expected that. "How big a blow?"

"You could risk the Strada project."

That took him aback. Giovanni knew from earlier cribbage night talks how important the project was, both to him and to the nation. He wouldn't throw out the comment lightly. "The latest polls had me somewhere between seventy-seven and seventy-nine percent favorable. That would take an awfully big blow."

"It could be a big blow, given that you're facing both the Aletta factor and the conflict of interest factor." Giovanni's mouth twisted. "Do you want my advice as your friend? Or as a disinterested party?"

"Are you disinterested?"

"I can fake it."

"You're my best friend and godfather to the crown prince. If you're able to successfully fake disinterest in my life, I'm in trouble."

"You're in trouble anyway." Giovanni raised a shoulder, then let it drop. "I think you should ask her. Let the ambassador make the decision."

"That sounds like advice from a friend."

"It's been a long time, Eduardo. You could have had any number of women warming your bed during those years. Or, as you say, visiting the palace under another pretense. You haven't."

"You don't know that."

"You haven't. You aren't wired that way. If you were, you wouldn't be the man who married Aletta Masciaretti. And you wouldn't be thinking about a woman like Claire Peyton now. So ask her."

Eduardo's mouth went dry. All of a sudden, the reality of asking Claire Peyton for a date made him nervous.

He wasn't a man prone to nerves.

Giovanni's mouth spread into a smile and he raised his empty tumbler. "In fact, we should toast to it. We have a fine New Mexico whiskey."

"Greta will crush me tomorrow."

"Greta will crush you tomorrow whether you drink or not."

"True." He looked at his tumbler. He hadn't the foggiest idea how he'd ask Claire for a date. Did he call the embassy? No, that wouldn't work. He'd have to get her number, which would be difficult without alerting the staff.

Even if he could figure out how to call her discreetly, would she agree? Where would they go?

He waved at the bottle. "Go ahead. Pour one for each of us."

CHAPTER 9

CLAIRE KNEW from the moment she chose a career in diplomacy that most Americans gave little thought to their state department, let alone their ambassadors. Their president, their senators and congressional representatives, sure. But not their ambassadors.

When they did think about ambassadors, or about the jobs ambassadors do, it was in terms of an individual ambassador's accomplishments. Were new business alliances established? Cultural ties strengthened? Did travel or trade become easier, or were health and educational initiatives created? A citizen might turn on the evening news, see the president deplaning in a foreign country, and being greeted by the ambassador at the airport. The president would then attend a press conference with that country's leaders and say, "Thanks to the hard work of Ambassador So and So, our two countries have forged a deeper relationship...."

Claire was used to most Americans having that image in their heads when a new acquaintance heard her job title. They had the idea that she was a forger of relationships. Or that she was the person who took the fall whenever a scandal erupted abroad.

Both of those facts were true.

They didn't grasp that she served as the public face of a large team of talented individuals who represented their nation and its interests in a particular country. A success wasn't her success, it was the team's success. And that team had several divisions: a political team, an economic team, a culture and education team. There were military experts and agricultural experts. An entire section was dedicated to helping U.S. citizens who encountered difficulties while abroad, whether that difficulty was as simple as a lost passport or as complex as being arraigned on criminal charges.

The success of an ambassador—and, therefore, of the mission— was all about the team. While some embassy staff changed with the election of a new president, others were part of an embassy's fabric and stayed for years. Richard Cartwright had assured her that the embassy in San Rimini possessed a solid staff. More and more, however, she'd come to believe that Richard had undersold them.

The embassy's staff was first rate.

Mark Rosenburg was one of those skilled staff members. Tonight, she'd discovered how astute and dedicated he was. He also had a sense of humor. She'd invited Mark and four additional members of his team to her home for a working dinner, during which they'd discussed the embassy's ongoing cultural exchange programs. She'd warned them that while the house had a table, chairs, and other furniture that came with the property, her dishes and flatware were still in boxes and it would be pizza night and casual.

Mark had offered to pick up pizza from a place called Pizzeria Fassina on his way. He'd arrived with his briefing notes, two large pizzas, enough salad to feed an army, and a caddy filled with napkins and flatware. "I brought these from home," he said, indicating the caddy as he'd set it on her table. "That way, we can eat salad with our pizza. But my wife wants it all back. Bummer, because I hate this pattern."

Claire had eyed it all and said, "We'll ensure she gets back every single fork. But I don't recall ordering salad."

"That's because you're new to town. You'll learn. If you order pizza from Fassina, you have to get the salad."

"Noted."

They'd spent the evening reviewing the embassy's current cultural exchange programs, then discussed a few ideas that had been tried in the past, but failed for one reason or another. Then she'd asked for everyone's thoughts on future programs or one-time events. Claire learned that the trip to Emory and the Centers for Disease Control was the result of Mark's initiative. After touring the University of San Rimini's School of Public Health and learning about their research the previous year, he'd made phone calls to Emory University and the CDC to propose a week-long exchange. The graduate students who'd participated had returned to San Rimini full of ideas. Students from Emory had learned about San Rimini's methods for handling emergency health situations and found ways to improve protocols in the United States.

It was exactly the type of program Claire wanted the embassy staff to pursue.

It had been a relaxing evening, particularly for a working dinner. There was an energy in the room Claire loved. Jokes were told, proposals batted around, and compliments paid, giving her the opportunity to learn more about the personalities of those on the staff. It was the type of atmosphere that could only come from having skilled people working on projects that spoke to their passions.

Delicious pizza and a spectacular salad capped it.

Afterward, Mark had stayed to help her clean. They'd hand washed the flatware and returned each piece to the caddy despite his protestations. "If you told my wife that it was irreparably damaged by some fault in your dishwasher, she'd believe you. Then I could buy something new. Something that doesn't look like it belonged to her great-grandmother Matilda."

"Did it?"

"No. We registered for it when we got married."

"So you were part of the decision?"

"Let's say that the wedding registry was my first diplomatic mission."

Claire had grinned. "But you're grumbling about it how many years later?"

"Six years, and never within earshot of my wife." He paused, then asked, "What's the lifespan of flatware?"

"Mark? Stick a fork in it."

They'd had a good laugh. Then she'd broached the subject of her Uganda initiative. She'd updated Mark on her meeting with the king as soon as Mark had returned from Atlanta and asked him to think about approaches for the four parliament members King Eduardo had mentioned.

At first, he'd been surprised at Eduardo's hesitancy, but when she'd told him about the Strada project, Mark had leaned back in his chair and whistled. "There's been talk for a year or two that King Eduardo would be the one to spearhead the project. Then we heard that members of his staff planned to meet last week with key interest groups from the Central Business District. Now that we know he's invested in making the changes, it puts a new spin on things. He'll be cautious."

Claire had nodded and they'd agreed to speak more tonight, after Mark had a chance to regroup from his trip.

As they crushed the empty pizza boxes, Mark said, "Sonia Selvaggi will be the toughest nut to crack. I've never met her, but I know her reputation. She's a former prosecutor and spent the first part of her career sending criminals to jail. Since she's been elected to parliament, she's voted for stricter punishments for a range of crimes and is the type to see evil everywhere. It's understandable, given that she's had dealings with some nasty people. As far as your program goes, she'll see the upside—that more education tends to drive down the crime rate—but she'll have concerns about teacher safety. She'll want to know how the teachers who work in these programs are protected when they're in rural villages. What access do they have to emergency services? What is their living situation? How does it vary from village to village? Who checks in on them?"

It was good information to have before making an approach. Mark had insights on the other parliament members Eduardo mentioned, plus a fifth, who could often be swayed on matters regarding educational programs outside the country. "You'll want that vote for insurance," he told her.

Then he surprised her by saying, "You must have made quite the impression. It took Ambassador Cartwright a solid two months before he had a private audience with King Eduardo following the presentation of credentials. When he did, it was a half-hour meeting in the palace office with the king's senior staff present. They eventually had dinners together and even met once or twice informally, but it took a long time."

Mark's tone was even as he spoke, but Claire felt the undercurrent. Mark wondered if there was something else going on, but didn't want to ask.

"I imagine the king's relationship with Ambassador Cartwright paved the way for me," she said as Mark wiped the table and she tackled the countertop.

"Perhaps, though you clearly did something right the night of the credentials ceremony. The purpose of Saturday night's dinner was for you to request a favor, not the other way around, and the invitation came from the king personally."

She paused and leaned one hip against the counter. "What are you saying, Mark?"

"I'm saying that you're more—" He hesitated, searching for the proper word, then settled on, "personable than Richard Cartwright in the eyes of the palace. Well, in the eyes of one particular person in the palace."

"And?"

"And, Madam Ambassador, you're handling it well so far."

She gave him a smile that let him know she understood his concern, as well as his reluctance to be more specific with his new boss. "Thank you, Mark. Noted."

"Noted." He grinned and returned a towel to the rack. "Like ordering salad at Pizzeria Fassina?"

"Exactly. I'm getting to know the lay of the land."

When they finished talking and he was ready to leave, she walked him to the door, wished him goodnight, then returned to the kitchen for a cup of tea. She usually did some reading before bed, but tonight her brain was worn out. Instead, she decided to sort through a box or two of her belongings and put things away.

"Eventually, every one of you will get unpacked," she said aloud to the stack of boxes sitting inside the kitchen.

She was trying to decide which box to tackle when she spied Mark's flatware caddy on the counter. Before she could pull up his number, she heard the distinctive buzz of the outer security gate. She went to the door and hit the button for the intercom. Sure enough, Mark had driven less than a block when he realized he'd left the flatware behind.

"I must still be tired from the trip to Atlanta," Mark said, a sheepish note in his voice as he climbed the front stairs to retrieve the caddy from Claire. "Glad I remembered before I got home. My wife would've thought I did it on purpose."

"When I meet her, I'll be sure to tell her that you did."

He laughed at that. As he backed down the front stairs, he added, "Let's hope I don't get a block away and realize I left a fork inside one of the pizza boxes."

"If so, I'll know you did that on purpose, because I counted them as they went back in the container."

She waved, then closed the door again.

Not five minutes later, the gate buzzed again. Claire stifled a laugh. She eyeballed the kitchen counter, but saw nothing. She returned to the front door, scanning the house as she went, then hit the button for the intercom.

"I told you, Mark, stick a fork in it."

"This is not Mark. I am here on behalf of King Eduardo."

She hesitated. "Excuse me?"

"I am here on behalf of King Eduardo with an invitation, Madam Ambassador."

She frowned. This wasn't right. If anyone from the palace needed her, they'd have communicated via the embassy. She'd have received a call, not a visitor at her gate.

It had to be Mark, giving her grief about the impression she'd made on the king. She appreciated his sense of humor, but this was pushing too hard on the issue.

"Mark, if you don't go home, I'll tell your wife you hid a spoon under the sofa cushion."

Silence came over the line. She waited. Finally, she said, "Mark?"

"Madam Ambassador, this is Miroslav Vulin. I am here on behalf of King Eduardo. I escorted you from your vehicle to the residence the night you dined with His Highness. I understand that this is irregular. If you would care to call the palace's main security office and ask for the chief of operations, you will be connected to Chiara Ascardi. She can verify my identity and current location. Once she does, I would appreciate it if you could come to the gate. I will wait."

The line clicked off.

Claire stepped back from the intercom. She wasn't caught off guard very often, but the quiet confidence in the masculine voice left her rattled.

She moved back into the house. A number of security cameras covered the exterior of the home and she could view the feed from a computer that was hidden in a closet near the front door. She'd listened carefully as the embassy's security team had instructed her on how to move from one screen to another, changing the view, but she hadn't had the opportunity to practice. It took her several seconds to pull up a visual of the front gate.

A dark car idled at the curb. Between the car and the gate stood a boulder of a man in a crisp suit.

She closed her eyes. It was the man who'd walked her to King Eduardo's apartment the night they'd had dinner together.

What had she said to him? To stick a fork in it?

She certainly didn't need to call the palace and ask for his location.

She went to the door, strode down the stairs, and opened the gate herself rather than push the lock release as she had for Mark.

"Madam Ambassador," Miroslav said, "that was a very quick phone call."

"I didn't need to call. My apologies, Miroslav. I was entertaining this evening and thought that a guest had returned."

The big man's brow furrowed. "And you wanted him to, ah, stick a fork in it? I have not heard that expression, but must assume it is not an expression of welcome."

"It was a joke."

At his silence, she prodded, "You said that you're here on behalf of King Eduardo. What may I do for you?"

"If you would oblige me and get in the rear seat, everything can be explained."

She didn't bother to hide her astonishment. "You want me to get into a car? Right now? I don't believe the embassy's security team would be happy with me if I did that."

"This is San Rimini and I work for His Highness. I assure you, you are perfectly safe."

She glanced up and down the street. The houses, most of which were behind gates similar to hers, were well-lit and occupied, but the sidewalk was silent. It was rare not to see anyone strolling home from dinner at one of the nearby restaurants or walking their dog along the tree-lined street following a long workday.

The combination of utter stillness that surrounded them and the idling car's high shine and tinted windows made her feel like she had stepped onto a movie set in the middle of the scene where bad things happened to the trusting heroine.

"Where is it you wish to go?" she asked. "If there's something you need to tell me, why can't you say it here?"

Miroslav reached for the door handle. "Please, Madam Ambassador."

She took a step backward, but stopped when she spied a pair of shiny black shoes and knees clad in dark slacks. Then King Eduardo leaned forward enough for her to see his face in the shadows of the rear seat.

"We don't need to go anywhere, Madam Ambassador," he said softly. "But if you have a moment, I would like a word."

CHAPTER 10

HE'D GONE about this all wrong.

Then again, Eduardo wasn't sure how else he could have done it. The biggest downside of his position was the utter lack of privacy. He couldn't exactly call the embassy and ask for the ambassador's personal number. Not without several members of Claire's staff—and his—finding out. Since Claire was both new to the country and a diplomat, he assumed it would be next to impossible for even his tech experts to track down her number. Nor did he have the option of grabbing a set of car keys, strolling out of the palace, and driving to the ambassador's residence like a normal person.

Involving Miroslav—and only Miroslav—was the most discreet approach he could conceive. Even so, Eduardo had the bone deep feeling he'd made an error.

Claire looked from Eduardo to Miroslav, then her gaze swept the street once more, as if gauging whether or not this was a prank. Finally, she moved forward and slid onto the seat beside him. Once Miroslav closed the door, she turned so she faced him. "Your Highness, forgive me. I didn't realize you were, well, *here*. I'd invited several staff members to the residence for a working dinner and they just left. When Miroslav rang, I thought one of them had come back."

"Miroslav parked down the street when he saw a car about to pull away from the curb in front of your house," he admitted. "We waited until he left and were about to take his spot when he returned."

"Mark Rosenburg. He forgot his flatware."

Eduardo blinked. "Flatware?"

"Mine isn't unpacked, so he brought some with him."

"I see." He didn't, but he wasn't sure it was important.

He'd rehearsed a half-dozen ways to do this in the car on the way here, but words failed him now. In the confines of the rear seat, Claire became flesh and blood rather than the woman who'd occupied his thoughts for the past several days. There were details—the silver bracelet at her wrist, the light scent of her perfume, the fact she'd dressed down from her office look by removing a jacket and rolling up the sleeves of her pink blouse—that didn't enter his mind when he daydreamed about her, and those details had him tongue-tied.

He was far more used to having others tongue-tied in his presence. He didn't like the sensation.

Worse, Claire was looking at him in expectation while Miroslav stood outside the car with his hands resting at his hips, monitoring the street as if he thought an assassin might leap from behind one of the trees at any moment.

If any of the neighbors stepped out to walk a dog or smoke a cigarette, Miroslav would scare them to death, even though the locals knew the residence was that of the U.S. Ambassador and subject to security monitoring.

The man had a gift for intimidation.

"I assume you have a purpose for this visit, Your Highness?"

"Yes."

"I can't wait to hear the cloak and dagger reason." Her smile was wide and her voice light, but her eyes held a hint of trepidation. "I hope you aren't here to renegotiate our deal. I have a meeting with Franco Galli on Monday. I'd hate to believe it's for naught."

"No. This is not in regard to our deal. Though when I told my staff about the deal at our Monday status meeting, I feared a rebellion."

"Sergio Ribisi?"

"And my press secretary. And a few others." Sergio had called in two other political consultants when Eduardo told his senior staff what had transpired at dinner. They'd come to the conclusion that the deal wouldn't matter, as Claire was unlikely to find support. Then his brain replayed what she'd just said. "You have a meeting with Franco Galli? Already?"

"Convincing four influential members of parliament to support a program takes time, particularly when they don't know me. I wanted to get the ball rolling."

"You chose wisely. I imagine that, of the four, Franco Galli will be the least difficult to convince."

"But not easy."

Eduardo acknowledged that with a tip of the head. "No, not easy."

"So if you aren't here to call off our deal...?"

Eduardo felt his smile falter. Even when caught unaware by press questions, he never felt this off kilter. "Have you seen *La Traviata?*"

"No, though I noticed it on the marquee at the Royal Theater."

"The final performance is next Saturday night. It's a fundraiser for the Royal Foundation of San Rimini, which supports a number of charities. I attend every year. Usually Princess Isabella accompanies me, but now that she's married, I've encouraged her to spend more time with her husband, rather than serving as my pity escort."

Claire's laugh was so sudden it seemed to surprise even her, since she quickly turned her face to the side.

"What?"

"Your Highness, I can't imagine anyone would consider themselves your 'pity escort,' even your daughter."

"I'm glad you think so, because that's the reason I came here. I'd like you to accompany me." He gestured in Miroslav's direction. "I didn't intend to make it a cloak and dagger invitation, but there are a number of obstacles to communicating with you directly."

"You want me to go to the opera with you?"

"Yes."

Her lips parted, but for a long moment, she said nothing. Her eyes swept over the console between the front seats, where his usual driver kept mints and bottles of chilled water within the king's reach. Then she met his gaze.

"Your Highness, is this—are you asking me—"

"I'm asking you for a date, Madam Ambassador, which is why I wasn't keen on going through both the palace and the embassy switchboards in order to reach you."

"Oh." Her eyes were full of questions, but she didn't ask any of them.

He wasn't sure what kind of reaction he'd expected, but an *oh* wasn't it.

He tried again. "I know that this could be viewed as a conflict of interest for you. Given that you're establishing yourself at the embassy, a date with me could be even more problematic. If you decline, I will understand. I won't take it personally." He felt one side of his mouth twist at the lie. "Well, I'll take it a little bit personally, but it won't affect our working relationship or our deal on your education program."

It took everything in him not to fidget as he waited for her response.

"Do you, ah, do you do this very often, Your Highness?"

"Have Miroslav stand guard while I ask an ambassador for a date? No. This is a first."

She made a face at his dodge. "I mean date. Do you date often? Because I'm wondering, given your position, how a date with you would work."

"Well, the basics probably work the same as for any other man. Small talk, dinner, some flirtation. But no, I don't date often. In fact, I haven't gone on a date in nearly a decade and that was with my wife. A date with me comes with public opinion attached. And possibly paparazzi. That's not an easy thing." He released a long breath. "If this all feels as uncomfortable for you as it does for me, please chalk it up to the fact that I'm out of practice. What about you?"

She glanced over her shoulder at Miroslav. Seeing that he hadn't moved, she repositioned herself in the seat so she faced him fully. "Being an ambassador makes dating a challenge, but probably not the challenge it is for you. I've managed a few. Mostly first dates, though, and none of those since I arrived in San Rimini."

"So we're both out of practice."

She arched a brow as if to say, *speak for yourself*. "Isn't *La Traviata* about a doomed relationship between a courtesan and a clueless nobleman?"

He made a show of looking suspicious. "I thought you hadn't seen it."

"I haven't, but I've seen *Moulin Rouge!* and it's my understanding that the movie followed the plot of the opera. Should I read anything into that?"

"Absolutely not. I'm inviting you to an event that happens to be at the opera. It's a fundraiser for a wonderful cause, one that's near and dear to my heart."

"Yes, I guessed you might have something to do with the royal part of the Royal Foundation." Her eyes narrowed, but there was a teasing quality to her expression. "I've never been to the opera before. Any opera."

"The Royal Theater is the perfect place to attend your first."

She smiled. "I like you, Your Highness. I'll go on one condition."

"Dates have conditions?"

"This one does."

He rolled his hand in a *let's hear it* motion, though hearing the two words *I'll go* tempted him to agree to anything she asked.

"Assuming we still like each other at the end of the evening, we make plans to see *Out of Africa*."

He wondered if Miroslav could sense his smile through the bullet-proof glass. "It's a deal."

"Sergio Ribisi won't like it any more than he liked your education deal."

"Probably not, but he'll have to live with it. Speaking of which, what did your staff say about the education deal?"

"They're supportive of my desire to involve San Rimini in the program and understand its importance to the President. Having a path to accomplish that goal that is good."

He angled his head at the odd note in her voice. "But?"

"I'm not sure they know what to make of the fact that I proposed the deal over a private dinner at the palace. It's not something my predecessor would have done."

Eduardo looked past Claire, toward the ambassador's residence. When he caught her gaze again, he said, "I imagine there are a lot of changes from one ambassador to the next. A good staff will adapt."

"I'm sure they will." Her lips curved. "Did you ever take Richard Cartwright to the opera?"

"Richard would have fallen asleep."

"I may, too. You never know."

"I do know." He wanted to touch her but resisted the urge. "Considering the hoops I needed to jump through to come here tonight without being seen, I should probably get your phone number."

She gave it and he added it to his phone, then grimaced. "Would it be a bad start to our date to ask you to meet me at the theater? I could send a car for you. It'd be less likely to draw attention than if I were to pick you up."

"I'd be happy to meet you there."

"I'll have my personal assistant greet you at the door and escort you to the royal box."

"The royal box? That sounds fancy, even for the opera. I'll be on my best behavior."

"No hiding whiskey in your handbag."

"I wouldn't dare." Her smile sent a thrill racing through him. "I'll see you there."

"I look forward to it."

She twisted to reach for the door handle, but slid on the leather seat and knocked her knee hard against his. On reflex, her hand went to his thigh, as if she could soften the blow. "Oh, I'm sorry, I—"

A flush rose from her neck to her cheeks and she yanked her hand away as if she'd accidentally reached into a snake pit. "Your Highness, I'm so—"

He caught her retreating hand. "Don't be sorry. For bumping into me or for this. I'm human, you know. Same as you. You won't catch fire if you touch me."

He rested both their hands against his knee.

They looked at each other for one beat, then two, and he realized that he was the one who could catch fire.

He leaned closer, then hesitated to gauge her reaction. Her eyes widened, but she didn't pull away. He closed the gap and kissed her. Slow, soft, easy. Her thumb moved over the back of his hand, then she kissed him back.

In that instant, it was as if his entire body exhaled. He moved his hand to cup her cheek, but didn't deepen the kiss. Much as he wanted to, the timing was wrong. This needed to be gentle. Romantic. And it was.

Even so, he felt her fighting to hold herself back as much as he was.

Eventually she eased away, but their foreheads remained close.

"I realize the windows are tinted, but Miroslav is going to wonder," she whispered.

"Miroslav is paid not to wonder. He does an excellent job of it."

"Don't be so sure. He strikes me as a man who sees and absorbs everything."

The observation made him smile. He gave her a final, quick kiss, then released her. "Before you go...what does 'put a fork in it' mean? When Miroslav went to the gate, I cracked the window so I could hear. I've never heard that phrase."

Amusement lit her face, though whether at the question or his attempt to lighten the mood, he wasn't sure. "What do you think?"

He considered. English wasn't his first language, but he'd spent enough time speaking it that he'd picked up a number of idioms. "I know 'put a sock in it' but not 'put a fork in it.' Do they mean the same thing?"

"Not quite. 'Put a sock in it' is a way of telling someone to stop talking."

"In a not-so-polite manner?"

TO KISS A KING | 101

"Correct. But when you're cooking meat, you might put a fork in it to see if it's done."

"So…you told Miroslav that he was done?"

"I thought I was telling Mark Rosenburg. It was a joke that related to something he'd said over dinner about forks. It just happened to be Miroslav at the intercom instead of Mark."

"I see. I assume you don't regularly tell callers to put a fork in it?"

"I don't tell anyone to put a fork in it."

"That would be poor diplomacy," he said, feigning seriousness.

"Extremely poor." One side of her mouth curved. "Speaking of diplomacy, I now have a beautiful symbol of friendship planted in a sunny spot at the back of the house. Thank you again for the olive tree."

"You're welcome. I'm glad you found a place for it." He directed a look at Miroslav's back. "Have a good night, Madam Ambassador. I'll see you next Saturday."

"Thank you for the invitation, Your Highness."

He wanted to tell her to call him Eduardo when they were alone, but before he could say it, she was out of the car. This time, without slipping on the leather seat.

It wasn't until she disappeared through the gate that the word *friendship* registered in his brain. Was she making a point by referring to the tree was a symbol of friendship?

He didn't want to be her friend. If the kiss they'd shared was one of friendship, then he was woefully out of practice.

Miroslav buckled his seat belt and put the car in gear, then checked the mirrors for oncoming cars. His gaze snagged Eduardo's and he raised a brow.

"Are we returning to the palace, Your Highness, or do you need to stop elsewhere?"

"La Rocca, please."

Miroslav nodded, then pulled into the street. Eduardo shifted to look out the window, but not before he caught sight of the big man's lower lip twitch into a smile.

CHAPTER 11

CLAIRE THANKED HER DRIVER, Fabiano, who offered her a hand as she stepped onto the sidewalk in front of the Royal Theater.

"You'll call afterward, Ma'am?"

"I will, thank you." She had checked with the theater the previous day to see what time the performance would end, but wasn't certain when she'd want to leave. Would King Eduardo have events to attend afterward? Would he need to network with Royal Foundation staffers, or meet the cast after the show? It wouldn't be uncommon for him to do so and she wasn't sure whether she should accompany him or not.

Fabiano was a friendly, squat, and heavily-muscled man in his fifties who'd grown up only a few blocks from the ambassador's residence, and had worked on the embassy's transportation staff for nearly thirty years. He'd been the one to drive Claire and Karen to the palace the night of her credentials ceremony, and he assured Claire that he was used to uncertain timing. "There's a café two streets away where I go whenever I'm on call in this area," he'd told her during their drive. "The owner is a cousin who allows me to park in his service alley on the condition I stay long enough for dinner. This qualifies."

Unfortunately, scheduling Fabiano meant involving Karen. Claire had waited until she and Karen were the last two people in the office on Thursday night before mentioning that she had an invitation to the final performance of *La Traviata* and needed to arrive twenty minutes prior to the curtain.

"Why twenty? Are you meeting someone? Should I arrange any security?"

"I'll be seated in the royal box. I'm arriving at the twenty-minute mark to meet an escort for security purposes."

They'd been partway to the elevator. Karen had stopped walking in the middle of the hall. "You're going to the opera. In the royal box."

"Yes."

It must not have come out in as offhand a manner as she'd hoped, because Karen had slow-blinked her disbelief. "Nothing came across my desk. Was I away when the call came through?"

"I received an invitation at the residence."

It was the closest Claire could come to making it sound official.

"That's odd. Did it come from the palace? Or from King Eduardo?"

Claire had gestured toward the elevator and started walking again, keeping a few steps ahead so that Karen couldn't read her expression. "The performance is a fundraiser for the Royal Foundation. Apparently Princess Isabella usually accompanies the king. Since she wasn't planning to attend this year, he asked if I would."

Everything she said was true, but it wasn't the whole story. Karen seemed to sense it. As they'd stood waiting for the elevator, Karen had changed her line of questioning to ask whether Claire had an appropriate dress unpacked.

"I have the green gown I wore to the Kennedy Center Honors a few years ago. That should work."

"Oh, I've seen photos of that. It will be perfect." They'd fallen silent until they were in the elevator, then Karen had asked, "I assume you haven't shared this with others on the staff?"

Claire had made a dismissive gesture, as if to say she saw no need.

"I'll call tonight and arrange transportation."

"Tomorrow will be fine. It's only from the residence to the Royal Theater and back."

The next morning, Karen told Claire what time to expect Fabiano at the residence. She didn't mention the opera date otherwise, and to Claire's knowledge, Karen hadn't breathed a word to the rest of the staff.

Not that Karen knew it was a *date* date. But given that Karen: a) was intelligent; and b) apparently hadn't informed the embassy's media specialists, it meant she harbored suspicions.

Typically, an ambassador accompanying a king to a public event constituted catnip for the embassy's public affairs staff, who'd want photos for the embassy website and press releases. But Claire hadn't heard a peep from them, which meant that, by default, Karen left the decision to inform public affairs to Claire.

Claire waited for Fabiano to leave the curb before she turned to take in the sight of the Royal Theater. She'd spent a few minutes that afternoon reading about its history. Built in 1800, it had taken the place of a much older theater and was designed to rival the performance halls that had recently opened in Vienna.

Judging from the exterior, the architect had accomplished the task.

Claire was halfway up the front steps when she heard a feminine voice say, "Madam Ambassador?" It took her a few seconds to find the source. A petite woman in an understated black strapless gown approached. Jet black hair swirled into a knot at her nape. She wore no necklace, but small diamond studs sparkled in her ears.

"I am Luisa Borelli, King Eduardo's personal assistant."

Claire shook the woman's hand. "It's a pleasure to meet you, Luisa. The king mentioned that you'd escort me to the box. Thank you."

"You're quite welcome. This way, Ma'am."

Inside, the decor was every bit as sumptuous as the theater's exterior promised. Stunning chandeliers glittered overhead, marble framed the entry doors, and rich red carpet covered the floor. Bartenders in immaculate suits manned bars at either end of the space while waitstaff circulated discreetly, trays at the ready to collect empty glasses. Though the doors to the theater stood open, most guests remained in the lobby with glasses of wine and champagne in hand as they socialized. Hundreds of voices swirled around her, their happiness turning the sound into a melody.

Luisa gestured toward one of the bars. "Would you care for a drink before we go upstairs? There are beverages in the box, but if you'd prefer to circulate first, you have a few minutes. I can wait for you by the staircase."

"No, thank you. I can go directly to the box."

They took the stairs to one of the upper levels. Luisa greeted a security guard, who signaled the ticket taker that the women could proceed. They followed a carpeted hall past several curtained archways, then approached a woman in a dark suit.

Luisa said, "Madam Ambassador, this is Chiara Ascardi. She is the head of palace security and will be on duty here in the hall during tonight's performance should you need anything."

"It's an honor to meet you," the woman said, shaking Claire's hand.

Claire gave Chiara a warm smile, then thanked both women for working on a weekend.

Chiara gave Luisa an amused look, then said, "It's not typical for either of us. But I love the opera, so this is a detail I don't mind coordinating." She indicated a closed door a few steps behind her, near the end of the hall. "This restroom is for the royal box. During the performance, I would prefer you come here rather than utilize the lobby facilities. Otherwise, please make yourself comfortable. His Highness should arrive shortly."

Claire thanked the security chief, then followed Luisa through the curtain and into the box.

Four plush chairs filled the small balcony. Beneath the rail, the velvet-covered wall boasted built-in drink holders and a sleek display shelf showcasing copies of the evening's program. It was as luxurious a spot as one could hope to occupy for the performance. However, as she approached the balcony rail, it was the sight of the theater's interior took Claire's breath away.

The layout was traditional, with a fanned area of seats, all of which appeared to have good views of the stage. The ceiling was painted to resemble the heavens, complete with dancing cherubs and fluffy clouds that glowed from the light of the sun. A single, massive chandelier dominated the center of the space. Intricate carvings fronted each of the balconies. She leaned forward for a better look and realized that they depicted scenes from classical plays. Directly across from her, Roman senators stabbed Julius Caesar. On the balcony beside that, Hamlet contemplated a skull. There were a few balconies with scenes she didn't recognize, then she spotted Lysistrata urging a group of women to withhold sex from their husbands in an attempt to stop the Peloponnesian War.

Luisa smiled as Claire's gaze moved from balcony to balcony. "The designs are original to the theater. They were all carved by hand."

"They're exquisite."

Luisa made a sound of agreement. "I take it this is your first visit?"

"It is."

"You're seeing it the proper way, then. There are floor seats with better views of the stage, but the box is more comfortable. It also allows you to see the balcony detail."

As Luisa spoke, the lights flashed and guests began making their way from the lobby to their seats.

"It's a marvelous spot for people watching," Claire said.

"Yes, and tonight's performance will be quite the fashion parade." Luisa's eyes tracked a chic woman with dark skin and a vibrant yellow gown as she made her way into the center of the third row. "The Royal Foundation fundraiser always draws a wealthy crowd who want an excuse to look their best. Thankfully, they also come with their pocketbooks open. After the final curtain, the cast will host a short auction to raise additional funds. The crowd gets into it and cheers on the bidders. There are autographed programs, photographs with the performers, and sometimes they'll offer props. Last year's Royal Foundation performance was *The Barber of Seville*, and the wedding contract between the Count and Rosina sold for quite a sum."

"Sounds like you've attended this event several times."

"Oh, yes, as long as I've worked for King Eduardo, but most years I don't watch the performance. I stay long enough to ensure His Highness doesn't need me, then I head home." No one was within hearing range, but Luisa dropped her voice. "I love this building and volunteer to do the pre-arrival inspection with the security staff any chance I get, but I'm not a fan of opera. That's why Chiara Ascardi gave me that look when you mentioned that we were both working on a weekend. Chiara knows I'd rather this fundraiser involved a big screen and a film packed with mindless humor. I only stayed for *The Barber of Seville* last year because it's a comedy."

Claire looked at Luisa. "You're staying tonight, though?"

She smiled and shook her head. "I have an appointment with a fluffy blanket and a fantastic romance novel."

Claire waved a hand to encompass Luisa's gown. "That's better than I've ever dressed for a blanket and a good book. Your gown is breathtaking. It's also perfectly suited to you."

"Thank you, Madam Ambassador. It's my favorite. Thankfully, given the king's public schedule, I have plenty of opportunities to wear it." Luisa's chin lifted suddenly. "Speaking of whom, I believe His Highness has arrived."

Sure enough, Claire heard King Eduardo's familiar voice coming from the corridor outside the box, most likely as he spoke with Chiara Ascardi. And damn if the sound didn't jack Claire's heart rate sky high.

For more than a week now, Claire had heard that same voice in her head, whispering the words he'd spoken just before he'd kissed her.

I'm human, you know. Same as you. You won't catch fire if you touch me.

Oh, how little he knew. Everything about Eduardo diTalora set her on fire. His voice. His gaze. And definitely his touch.

Thankfully, it didn't take a diplomat's perception to realize that she had the same effect on him.

What they would do about it, though, that she didn't know.

The next few minutes passed in a blur. The theater lights flashed once more, the remainder of the guests hurried from the lobby to take their seats, then King Eduardo entered the box as the lights dimmed. He said something to Luisa as she passed him on her way out, then took a step toward Claire and leaned in so she could hear him over the swell of murmurs from the crowd below.

"I'm glad you're here." Even in the faint light, his eyes twinkled. "I need to go on stage for a moment. Have a seat and I'll be right back. If you'd like a drink, there's a refrigerator hidden behind the seats."

He disappeared through the curtain. She glanced behind her and noted a low cabinet with a built-in refrigerator unit. Through its glass door, she saw several bottles of water and soda along with what appeared to be a bottle of wine. Four highball glasses and four wine glasses were arranged beside an ice bucket on top of the cabinet.

Luisa was right about this being the proper way to see the opera.

Claire slipped into a seat, then a spotlight tracked across the stage and the crowd silenced. The king stepped into the spotlight and a wave of applause rose from the seats. Claire realized that he must have taken a staircase that connected their hallway to an area backstage.

The king welcomed the audience to the performance and noted that the proceeds of the evening's ticket sales went to the Royal Foundation of San Rimini. He thanked the cast, crew, and theater staff for donating their time and talents, then said, "The Foundation supports a wide array of charities and philanthropic causes, from preserving our country's architectural wonders—such as this very building—to protecting our historic waterfront from the effects of pollution and climate change. The goal of the Foundation is to ensure that future generations have the opportunity to enjoy San Rimini's splendor. It is my honor to be here tonight and to share this evening with you. I hope you will stay after the curtain call for a special event that will be presented by the cast. And now, *La Traviata*."

The spotlight faded and the king moved offstage. The curtain rose on the scene of a lavish Parisian salon decked out for a party. As the opera began, King Eduardo eased into the seat beside Claire's.

Softly, he asked, "How did I do?"

"You're a natural performer."

He smiled, then looked toward the stage. The main character, a stunning courtesan named Violetta, had entered the salon to applause from the audience.

Claire shifted so the king could hear her. "This will test my Italian."

"Focus on the music. It's transporting in any language."

At first, Claire sat as she usually did when in public: back straight, legs crossed at the ankles, hands folded in her lap. Though the production was mesmerizing, she was keenly aware of the audience sneaking peeks at the royal box. But Eduardo was right. The music was truly transporting, filling the theater and wrapping the audience in a magical bubble of sound and emotion. Knowing the story ahead of time was helpful, but Claire believed she'd have been able to follow the action regardless. When the performers began what was obviously a drinking song, she found herself relaxing in the seat.

Eduardo leaned closer, his shoulder brushing hers. "You're smiling."

"So are you."

Before Claire knew it, Violetta captivated the house with a song about needing her freedom, the stage lights dimmed, and the curtain fell to end the first act. The audience cheered.

She and Eduardo both stood and clapped, joining the rest of the crowd.

"Come with me," Eduardo said, then cradled her elbow and led her from the box as the theater lights rose. Chiara stood near the curtain, preventing anyone who might be exiting the other boxes from approaching. Eduardo led Claire past the restroom, then through a second door to a narrow staircase.

"I assume this leads to the stage?"

"It does. But there's something else I'd like to show you." They went down a short flight of stairs, but instead of turning at the landing and continuing their descent, Eduardo pulled aside a wall covering to reveal a hidden door. He turned the knob, then reached for her hand. "Are you bothered by heights?"

"No."

"Good, because you'll love this."

CHAPTER 12

EDUARDO CLOSED the door behind her. As Claire's eyes adjusted to the darkness, she saw why he made it sound as if they were embarking on an adventure. "Is this the catwalk?"

He flashed a grin more suited to a mischievous child than a monarch. "Want to take back what you said about heights?"

"Never."

"Watch your heels. They could get caught."

His fingers tightened around hers as he eased her onto a metal-grated walkway with railings on either side that allowed them to see all the way to the floor. He stopped over the wings in a spot that offered a view of the entire stage. Below them, the crew moved with the precision of a military unit as they whisked away chairs and giant candelabra and replaced them with set pieces for the next scene. The hum of voices from the audience carried through the curtain, which remained closed for intermission, but in the lofty space where Claire and Eduardo stood, all was silent.

He turned so they stood side by side and encouraged her to lean over the railing, but his hand remained wrapped around hers. He kept his voice low so they wouldn't be heard by the crew. "I thought you might want to see what goes on behind the scenes."

"I love this. Thank you."

She meant it. There was something both fascinating and romantic about seeing the stage from above. Then there was the man beside her. Eduardo diTalora possessed a gravitas that came from within, rather than from his title. She could have met him in a grocery store or while walking through a city park, have known nothing about his background, and been drawn to him after exchanging only a few words.

"I'm glad you're enjoying the performance, even if Italian isn't your first language."

"You say that as if it's my second. It's not. I'm frantically teaching myself in the evenings when I get home from the office."

"How is it going?"

"Slowly. I took Spanish through high school and college, which helps. There are enough similarities between the words and sentence construction that I can figure out most of what I read and some of what I hear. Speaking is another matter. That will take time."

"How is your adjustment to San Rimini going otherwise?"

"It's been smooth. The residence is stunning and I'm mostly unpacked. I've also discovered that I was gifted with an amazing staff. They're intelligent, interesting people, and we've been able to continue projects started during Ambassador Cartwright's tenure without missing a beat." She briefly told him about an American telecom company she'd assisted with a regulatory concern and a family the embassy had reunited after a passport issue.

"How about you?" she asked. "How has your project for the Strada il Teatro been going?"

He gave her an update on meetings that had taken place between his staff and the business district's various interest groups. "It's diffi-cult to find common ground given their wide range of concerns, but Sergio assures me that we're making progress."

"Let me guess: every group wants another group to compromise?"

"Exactly."

She smiled. Below them, the crew wrapped up preparations for the second act. Eduardo glanced at his watch and noted that they had a few more minutes before they needed to return to their seats. "Do you need to use the restroom?"

She shook her head. His fingers tightened around hers. Their hands were on the railing now. Being alone with him in such a setting was thrilling, yet oddly comfortable at the same time.

"What did Sergio think of tonight?" she asked.

"Do you mean the fact that we're on a date?"

"Yes."

"Nothing, because I didn't tell him."

Claire didn't bother hiding her surprise, which drew another mischievous look from the king.

"I have a senior staff meeting every Monday morning. When it came time to review my schedule this week, I merely confirmed my attendance tonight. Luisa and my security team know that you're here, obviously, but I did not inform them that this is a date." He cast a glance at the closed curtain. "However, Margaret Halaby, my Director of Charities and Patronages, is seated in the second row. I saw her look at the box more than once during the performance. She'll have questions at this Monday's meeting. She'll pose them more delicately than Sergio or my press secretary will, though."

"I've seen your press secretary. I don't think delicate is in Zeno Amendola's nature."

"No. I don't think anyone with shoulders as mountainous as his is capable of delicate."

There was affection in his voice as he mentioned his staff. She gave him a questioning look. "Do they ask because they're curious or because they worry it will affect your public role?"

"Probably a little of both. It's human nature. However, it's also their job and they're exceptional at what they do." His thumb moved over the back of her hand. His eyes followed the movement for a moment, then he tilted his head to study her. "What about you? Did you tell your staff?"

Claire shrugged. "On Thursday I told my assistant that I was invited to the royal box for the opera and asked her to make arrangements for a driver. When she questioned why she hadn't heard about it, I told her the invitation came to the residence."

"You dodged."

"Poorly, I'm afraid. Karen knows it's a date, but is pretending like she doesn't."

That drew a laugh from the king. "You wanted to see how tonight went before saying anything. You were a chicken."

"I could accuse you of the same thing."

"And it would be true." He angled his body so they were facing one another, but didn't release her hand. "I don't tell my senior staff everything. For instance, they didn't know that I'm going to be a grandfather again until about an hour before Marco and Amanda made their announcement on Wednesday."

"I saw that. Congratulations."

"Thank you. I'm excited for them." His eyes crinkled at the edges. "I'm excited for myself. I love Arturo, Paolo, and Gianluca. Being a grandparent makes me happier than I ever would have believed. The point is, my life is public. I fully understand why the people of San Rimini feel they have a right to know what I do. I even understood the demand for details when I had heart surgery. But the few parts of my life that are justifiably private I work hard to keep that way. I couldn't maintain my sanity otherwise. I need time to be myself. To laugh with my children and grandchildren and not have the world bear witness to it."

"When you invited me on this date, I seem to recall your insistence that you're human."

"Do you believe me?"

"I'm getting there," she teased. "You do have that whole larger-than-life quality."

"Says the ambassador."

"Not the same as a king."

They were quiet for a long moment. "I'm old enough to know my heart and my mind. And I'm old enough not to play games. So I'll be direct. I want to see more of you, Claire. I want to spend time—real time—talking to you. Like this, where we can be candid. Where you can call me Eduardo instead of Your Highness. I'd like to take you to other events. To share dinners that aren't about political or economic matters if we don't want them to be. Where we can talk about our families and movies and books or discuss the qualities of whiskey from New Mexico versus Tennessee versus Scotland."

"You don't have friends for that?"

"I do. I imagine you do, too. But it's not the same."

"No, it's not," she admitted. The lights flashed and a rush of sound came from the other side of the curtain. The stage below them stood empty. In less than a minute, the performers would take their places for the beginning of the second act. From somewhere backstage came the sound of a soprano warming up. It made both of them smile.

Eduardo pulled her close and they listened. Claire closed her eyes, breathing in all that surrounded her: the warm, spicy scent of Eduardo's skin. Dust from the heavy stage curtains. Wax from the floorboards far below. She allowed her head to drop against his shoulder and her hands to skim the back of his jacket.

She'd thought the performance had encased them in a magical bubble. This surpassed it.

"Seeing me on a personal level could be a risk for your career," he said quietly. "But I believe that the more we get to know one another, the more we'll find we have in common. In the meantime, we can work together to mitigate pressure from the media, should that become an issue."

"I would like that. Well, not the career risk. But the rest." She eased back enough to make out his features. "You should know, though, that there's no discussion on the whiskey front. I'm going to stand up for my home state."

"We'll see about that."

The kiss they shared warmed Claire all the way to her bones. A creak from the far side of the stage was quickly followed by a vibration underfoot as someone moved onto the opposite end of the catwalk.

"That's our cue," Eduardo said. "Time for the second act."

As the curtain rose onstage, Eduardo and Claire slipped into the box. Before long, the music enveloped them.

Then Eduardo reached for her, holding her hand below the line of the balcony.

EDUARDO PAUSED JUST inside the curtain at the rear of the royal box.

The woman who'd played Violetta stood onstage, holding the necklace she'd worn for the role. As bids came in, she sweetened the pot by offering a signed poster in which she was shown wearing the piece.

The audience was riveted on the woman, who knew exactly how to engage a crowd. Eduardo had eyes only for Claire. She sat where he'd left her at the end of the performance, leaning forward to take in the sights and sounds of the theater. He'd gone backstage to greet the cast and crew as the auction took place and to thank them for all they were doing to raise awareness of the Royal Foundation and its purpose.

As if she sensed his presence, Claire turned in her seat. Her smile made his throat catch.

He moved forward and into the seat beside hers.

"This is the final item. If we want to leave unnoticed, now's the time. Chiara has a car waiting in the alley behind the theater. We can go to a trattoria I know of a few blocks from here. We'll have privacy."

"I should let my driver know. He's waiting in a café nearby."

"I could have my driver return you to your residence after we leave the trattoria if yours wants to get home, but that might raise questions."

"I'll call him on our way out."

Claire's driver had told her that it was no problem to be in front of the trattoria whenever she wished. "This is early for me," he assured her. "I work evenings and never sleep before two or three."

"Thank you, Fabiano. Do you want me to get you anything at the trattoria? Maybe a dessert?"

"No, no. I have plenty. Enjoy yourself. It's no problem."

Soon they were settled at a table at the rear of the restaurant, in a spot that allowed them to eat without being seen by the rest of the dining area. The owner, whom Eduardo had known since he was young, had long since retired, but his daughter, Gaia, greeted the king as if he were a member of her family.

"I have fresh raspberry tarts, or a tiramisu, if you'd prefer."

Eduardo glanced at Claire. She told Gaia, "I'm a fan of raspberry tarts, but I suspect His Highness would prefer the tiramisu."

"How'd you guess?" he asked, though he was thinking of the cake and berries he'd complained about during their palace dinner and knew she was thinking of it, too.

Gaia looked from Claire to the king. "Is Samuel still feeding you bird seed and berries?"

"He is."

"You need extra, then."

"A small serving is plenty, but definitely the tiramisu rather than the tart. Thank you, Gaia."

For the next hour, he and Claire talked about their families. Eduardo confided that Amanda's doctor was fairly sure she was having a girl. "There are a number of downsides to my job, but the biggest upside is that the palace is large enough that my adult children can live under its roof while still maintaining their own households. I know my three grandsons as if they were my own children. I expect the same will be true with my granddaughter. Whenever I'm annoyed by the public nature of my role or I have a day where the weight of my responsibilities exhausts me, I think of my grandchildren. What about you? Where is your family?"

"They're in New Mexico, in a mountain town called Chama near the border with Colorado. My father's parents ran a hotel there that primarily caters to hikers, cyclists, and fishermen. When they retired, my dad's sister took over. My parents run a towing and auto repair business nearby. You'd be stunned at the number of travelers who show up in town with automotive issues."

"Was your mother raised there, as well?

Claire shook her head. "She was born on a Navajo reservation near the Four Corners area."

"Your mother is Native American?"

"Proudly so. Unfortunately, her parents were dirt poor and her father died of complications from alcoholism when my mother was a baby. If you want to know why I'm so invested in educational programs, it all comes from my mother. She was able to participate in Head Start, which is a program that ensures children from low income families begin school on equal footing with their peers. Her life would have been drastically different without it. She and her two older brothers worked hard and all three graduated high school with honors. That education—that opportunity—helped them rise out of poverty. My mother was awarded a scholarship that enabled her to attend a community college for two years, then she finished her economics degree at the University of New Mexico. One of my uncles still lives on the reservation and teaches third grade in a Navajo school in Shiprock. The other runs his own plumbing business."

He wasn't sure what he'd expected her to say but it wasn't this. The sharp difference from his own background fascinated him. "You have a lot of respect for her."

"For both of my parents. I try to channel their work ethic into everything I do. Anything I've accomplished is because of them."

At the love in Claire's voice, he fell a bit harder for her. "They must be proud of you, too."

"They are. My mother even set up an alert so she knows when I'm mentioned in a news report online. She called when she saw an article about the credentials ceremony. She was very excited that her daughter met a king. Her first question was, 'Is he as handsome in real life as on television?'"

"And you said?"

"I believe I laughed at the question."

The flirtation in her voice made Eduardo's insides clench with want, but rather than lean closer and kiss her, he smiled in return and said, "Next time, tell them I'm better in real life."

"Maybe I will."

As they finished dessert, the conversation turned to their upcoming work schedules. Then Claire noted that she'd had a productive talk with Franco Galli. "I think I have him convinced that the education program works, but he hasn't fully committed to it. I have a meeting with Monica Barrata next week and Franco said he wanted an update on how that meeting goes. I think if I can convince one of them, I'll convince the other. My staff says they have similar philosophies and that their votes rarely differ."

"I hope you convince them both, then."

She eyed him over the last bite of her tart. "Really? Even if it means you'll have to spend some of your valuable political capital?"

He liked that she had the backbone to tease him. "You have to get all four. That was the deal."

"Two is halfway."

He didn't point out that Franco Galli and Monica Barrata were the easiest votes of the four. As Claire set her fork across her plate, he winked and said, "Let me know when you convince all four."

"I'll do that."

After notifying their drivers and paying the bill—over Gaia's objection—they made their way to the front of the trattoria. It was closing time and the last of the customers had departed a few minutes earlier. To his relief, Gaia disappeared into the kitchen, giving them a few valuable moments alone.

He stopped Claire just short of the door, keeping them out of sight of the street. "I enjoyed this."

"So did I."

The sincerity in her voice made him as happy as he'd been in a long time. When he pulled her close and kissed her, her fingers curled around his elbow and an entirely different emotion swept through him. He held her as long as he dared.

Stolen moments were just that—moments—and perhaps that was part of their magic. He craved more.

"We'll do this again soon?" he murmured near her ear.

"Maybe something that doesn't involve high heels. Or two drivers and a staff to pull off."

"Like a movie?" he asked. "I believe we had an agreement to see *Out of Africa*. I have an engagement on Friday night that Luisa can move if you're free then."

"It's a date."

"Come to my place," he said, giving her a final, quick kiss. "It's cleaner than most bachelor's apartments, I promise."

"I seem to remember that."

He waited a full minute after her car was gone before slipping out of the trattoria and into the back seat of his own car. He allowed his eyes to drift closed for the brief, dark drive through the city streets, imagining the feel of Claire Peyton in his arms and the taste of her on his lips.

CHAPTER 13

CLAIRE GREETED the guard as she passed through security at the embassy's employee entrance, then made her way to the elevator. Her footsteps echoed against the marble as she walked. At quarter to seven, the streets had been quiet, save for a few runners and cyclists, and the embassy was empty.

Given her packed week, it made sense to arrive early, but Claire hadn't needed her alarm clock this morning. She'd been on an adrenaline rush since Saturday night's opera date with King Eduardo and had awakened an hour earlier than usual, brimming with energy. She planned to make the most of it.

After stopping by her office to drop off her bag and a stack of reports she'd brought home to review, she made her way to the small break room down the hall to start a pot of coffee. To her surprise, Karen stood at the counter, her back to the door as she spooned ground coffee into a paper filter.

"Good morning," Claire said as she entered. "You're in early."

Karen measured out another scoop without looking up. "So are you, Madam Ambassador."

Claire grabbed the empty pot and walked to the sink to get water while Karen plugged in the machine. After Claire added the water and set the pot in place, Karen started the brew cycle. It was a system they'd worked out during their years in Uganda, when they'd often arrived for work at the same time, each craving a morning cup of java. As Karen sealed the bag and replaced it on the shelf, she asked, "You didn't get any on your way? I'm used to you arriving with a cup in hand from one of the cafés down the street."

"I woke up wired and decided to come straight to the office. Besides, now that I've satisfied my curiosity and tried all the coffee places between here and the residence, my wallet will be happier if I stick to the break room most days."

Karen said, "ah," but didn't quite meet Claire's gaze. They'd known each other long enough for Claire to realize something was off. She asked if everything was all right, but Karen merely shrugged and turned toward the table where she'd left her tote bag. She withdrew a container—presumably her lunch—and slid it into the refrigerator.

Something was definitely off. Claire tried again. "Did you have a good weekend?"

"I did."

"Settled in the flat?"

"Yes. Even did some baking yesterday. I ran into someone I met during our first week here while I was buying flour. We started talking and it turns out his sister runs a bakery. He came over and showed me how he makes croissants."

"That sounds intriguing."

"Just making a new friend and improving my croissants."

"Ah."

At this point on a typical Monday, Karen would usually ask about Claire's weekend. Today, she didn't.

"Oh, good morning," a male voice came from the doorway. "Karen, Madam Ambassador. I didn't realize either of you were in the building already."

Claire turned to see John Oglethorpe. As Public Affairs Officer, John served as her senior advisor on public affairs and public diplomacy. He oversaw both the embassy's resource information center and its press office, which arranged press conferences, briefings, and interviews. He'd been the one to bring her up to speed on the public relations initiatives that had taken place during Richard Cartwright's tenure and kept her updated on San Rimini's reactions to news and events in the United States. After nearly a decade at the embassy, he knew all the players in the local media. During their initial meetings, she'd found him both shrewd and insightful.

Claire welcomed him with a smile. "Busy week ahead. Are you usually here before seven?"

"I like to catch the early morning news programs and papers in case anything needs to be addressed. No surprises that way."

Karen shouldered her tote and moved to the door. "I'll drop this at my desk and be back when the coffee's finished."

"Have you turned on a television this morning?" John asked once they were alone.

"I haven't, no. I arrived a few minutes ago and made a beeline for the caffeine."

John looked over his shoulder, as if checking to ensure no one was in the hallway. "You went to the opera on Saturday night and were seated beside the king in the royal box."

"Yes."

"You don't think I should have heard about that from you, rather than seeing it on the morning news?"

She froze. "You're kidding me. The morning news?"

He didn't roll his eyes, but his expression said as much.

She raised a hand. "I know, I know. I probably should have expected it."

John glanced into the hallway again, then moved further into the break room. "Any engagements involving the diTalora family draw the media. In the future, I'd appreciate it if you would inform me ahead of time so I can prepare a response in advance of any press inquiries."

"Have you received any yet?"

"I had six calls before breakfast yesterday and at least another dozen during the day. I haven't listened to my messages yet this morning, but there are a lot of them. When I passed by a news kiosk on my way in, I saw the latest *Today's Royals* with a photo of you and King Eduardo on the front. I don't know what it says because I didn't want to be seen buying a copy, but I'll have someone do so discreetly later."

A choice four-letter word sat on the tip of Claire's tongue at the mention of the gossip rag, though if she'd actually said it, it would have been directed at the situation, not at John. He had the respect of everyone in the embassy. She'd seen it in people's expressions and body language any time John walked by their desks or ran into them in the elevator. And in this case, he was right to be frustrated.

She leaned against the counter and crossed her arms. She'd thought when she'd spotted theatergoers looking into the royal box, there might be a call or two from a tabloid, but nothing like this. "I'm sorry, John. I didn't intend to place you in a difficult situation."

"I appreciate that. In any event, I wanted to talk to you before I respond. I need to ensure that our messaging is clear. Nothing I say can conflict with any public statements you may have made."

"I haven't said a word."

"All right. Well, that's good." John exhaled, apparently relieved Claire hadn't failed to notify him about any interviews. "Once the coffee is ready, we should find an office and discuss what you want said about the embassy's support of the Royal Foundation. Anything about how the partnership came about and why you were in the royal box would quell gossip and focus on our two countries' mutual goals, the importance of the Foundation and its work, et cetera."

It was Claire's turn to exhale. A beep sounded from the coffee machine. She offered John a cup. When he waved it off, she poured one for herself. Quietly, she said, "There's no partnership."

He absorbed that for a moment. "Maybe I will have a coffee. Preferably with bourbon."

She smiled at his attempt to lighten the moment, then took a tentative sip of her coffee to test its temperature. "I was in the box because I received a private invitation from King Eduardo. It came to the residence, not the embassy, which is why I didn't mention it to you. I only told Karen on Thursday evening so she could make arrangements for secure transportation, the same as I would if I'd decided to go to Venice to see St. Mark's or take a shopping trip to Trieste over the weekend."

"You're saying it was a date."

She paused. She wasn't ready to share it with the world, but she owed John the truth. "Yes. It was a date."

"Wow. Just...wow." John blinked, then shoved his hands into his front pockets. "That explains a lot. It also means there's little our office can say. I can't tell the media that you were there in your official capacity to support the objectives of the Royal Foundation and its work."

"I realize that."

"But I need to say something. Silence means they'll create a story to fill the void."

"I realize that, too." She quieted as two people walked past the break room door. They were deep in conversation and didn't notice that John or Claire were inside, let alone the tension that permeated the room. Once the pair had moved out of hearing range, Claire said, "Let's see what the coverage looks like as the day goes on, then we'll decide what to say. If you've received inquiries, I imagine the palace information offices have, as well. They may have already made a statement."

John nodded, but didn't look appeased.

"What is it?" she asked.

"I need to say something, Madam Ambassador, but I'm not sure I'm adept enough to manage it without offense."

"You're the Public Affairs Officer. 'Adept speaker' is in the first line of your job description."

"This is new territory." He shifted as if gathering himself, then focused on her. "You're single. You can date whomever you please, and everything I've ever heard about the king indicates that he's a good man and one of the few around whose intelligence is on par with yours. But King Eduardo is not simply a good man, he's a national symbol. Unless this relationship goes all the way, and I mean *all* the way, you're going to have fallout. He won't be the one to pay the price. You will. And if you do, that will be hard on every single person who works under this roof, both personally and professionally."

"John—"

"I should go to my office now. I'll catch up on messages, do a bit of reading, and see what the palace has said, if anything. Can you meet me in the conference room for lunch? Say, twelve-thirty?"

"I have a meeting scheduled with Monica Barrata at two in her parliament office. If we can finish by one-thirty, that will work."

"Are you seeing her about the Ugandan education program?"

At Claire's nod of confirmation, he said, "I might be able to use that. I'll see you at twelve-thirty."

He brushed his hand over his head as he strode out the door, as if doing so might clear the conversation from his mind.

"Good morning, Your Highness. Did you enjoy your session with Greta this morning?"

Eduardo gave Luisa a hard stare as he met her at the bottom of the stairs. She was always chipper on Mondays, but had an extra bounce to her step today. "Of course not."

"In that case, I'm sure it was quite productive. She told me it was a thruster day. I have no idea what that means, but it sounds like fun."

He greeted one of the guards as they strode toward his office. It was only eight a.m., and already his hamstrings and quads were sore from the morning's workout. Once they were clear of the guard, he told Luisa, "For your information, a thruster is when you pick up a loaded barbell in what's called a clean." He demonstrated by holding his hands in front of his shoulders, palms up and elbows pointing forward. "You catch it in a full squat, then straighten and thrust the bar overhead while keeping your core engaged. With Greta, you do a lot of those in a row. I may not be able to walk by the end of the day."

"You'll feel better knowing that you have the best muscle tone of any sitting monarch."

"I may not be able to sit, either."

She handed him a piece of paper. "This is your schedule for the day. Zeno asked to extend the morning status meeting. I gave him an extra fifteen minutes and moved your haircut to four-thirty."

He frowned. "Wasn't I meeting with Prince Antony this afternoon? He has a major fundraiser for the San Riminian Scholarship fund next week and wanted input on his speech."

She gestured to the paper. "I gave him a thirty-minute block prior to your haircut."

They turned a corner that brought them within sight of King Eduardo's office. There were several couriers waiting at Luisa's desk, all holding paperwork that required her signature. To Eduardo, she said, "I'll have your coffee in a moment, Your Highness."

Eduardo wished the couriers a good morning before entering his formal office, where Sergio, Zeno, and Margaret waited. Margaret's yellow notepad had more scribbles than usual.

The group surged to their feet and wished him good morning. Luisa closed the door behind him and he rounded the desk while gesturing for everyone to relax. "Word of warning: I had a difficult session with Greta this morning, then Samuel Barden served fruit pie for breakfast. While fruit pie sounds delicious, I don't think it had a single gram of sugar and the crust was made of oatmeal. Or something that resembled oatmeal. Tell me something that will restart my week on a positive note."

Zeno and Sergio both looked to Margaret. Eduardo followed suit, wondering what they expected her to say.

Her mouth twisted. "I, uh, just told Zeno and Sergio that when I arrived this morning Samuel offered me fruit pie."

"And you said?"

"I said yes. And after I ate it, I said, 'yum.' It was fabulous."

Luisa entered with his coffee, then placed it at his elbow. After she slipped out, he said, "You all look anxious to speak, so we'll hold the fruit pie debate for later. If it's something other than the Strada il Teatro project, let's hold on it. We're down to nine weeks before parliament needs a finalized plan in hand. And that's at the latest if we want to ensure it's part of their budget discussion for the Central Business District."

Looks were exchanged, then Sergio said, "I can give the Strada update, but it ties into another matter, so they need to be discussed together."

"Which is?"

Sergio's eyes flicked to Zeno, who said, "The Claire Peyton situation."

CHAPTER 14

EDUARDO'S GUT TIGHTENED. He made a conscious effort not to show it. "There's a Claire Peyton situation? I'm unaware of a Claire Peyton situation, let alone how one might relate to the Strada il Teatro."

He said it in a tone meant to end discussion, but Zeno forged ahead. "The morning news reported that the ambassador attended the opera with you on Saturday and was seated in the royal box. We" —he made a circle with his index finger to encompass everyone in the room— "didn't see her mentioned on the schedule. The usual royal tabloids have speculated wildly about the reason—"

"As they always do."

"Yes, Your Highness. So far, the mainstream outlets have steered clear of speculation. However, one of the high-circulation tabloids indicated that members of the backstage crew were overheard in the alley behind the theater saying that during the intermission, the king was on the catwalk above the stage holding hands with a mystery woman later identified as Claire Peyton." Zeno visibly reddened as he said it, but his voice remained even.

"And this affects the Strada project...how?"

"It's a problem, Your Highness, because the gossip is out there," Sergio said. "Even if Zeno avoids the topic in this morning's press briefing so as not to call attention to it, every other outlet is now looking for it."

"Men and women have been known to see each other socially, Sergio, particularly single men and women."

Eduardo didn't miss the look of surprise on the faces of his senior staff. They hadn't expected him to confirm that the night was, in fact, a date.

Sergio folded his hands in his lap, then quickly unfolded them and leaned forward. "It's my job to give you the truth, even when it's hard to do so. Part of your popularity lies in the fact that you are single. It gives you a certain mystique. If that changes—even with a woman whose reputation is as good as the ambassador's—it will affect everything you do."

"Wait a minute. You're saying that *going on a date* will hurt my popularity, and therefore hurt our ability to unify support for the Strada project before we hit the deadline to put it in front of parliament? That's a stretch, don't you think?"

Even as Eduardo said the words, he envisioned Giovanni sitting across the cribbage board from him, warning him that his popularity would take a hit.

Of course, then Giovanni had said, "you're in trouble anyway," and urged him to ask Claire for the date.

"I'm looking ahead," Sergio said. "Anyone with a vested interest in the Strada project will do the same. Groups who have been brainstorming ways to push back against aspects of your plan may be tempted to wait and see how this plays out rather than come to the table. If your popularity were to dip, they'll take advantage of that fact to ask for more concessions."

Eduardo drummed his fingers on the desk, then said, "Point made. Let's cross that bridge when we come to it, shall we?"

"There's also the agreement you made with the ambassador, Your Highness. You said you'd introduce legislation to parliament regarding support for her education program if she harnessed certain votes."

Eduardo gave a roll of his hand, urging Sergio to continue.

"When you told us about it last week, my consultants didn't believe the deal would matter. They doubted the ambassador could find the support to hold you to it. But that's changing. We understand that the ambassador is meeting with Monica Barrata today. She met with Franco Galli last week and the word is that he came away leaning toward the program. If he supports it, Barrata is also likely to give it her support. They tend to vote in lockstep."

"She'd still need Luciano Festa and Sonia Selvaggi. They'll be far more difficult to convince."

"I agree, those two will be tough. Particularly Selvaggi. But I wanted to raise the concern. There are a lot of moving pieces to this project. We need to control what we can."

Eduardo took longer than usual to respond. When he did, his voice broached no argument. "I won't put the Strada project at risk."

There was a collective, "Yes, Your Highness."

Eduardo addressed Zeno. "Should the subject arise, Claire Peyton is the United States Ambassador to San Rimini. As such, she has frequent interaction with the palace, with parliament, and with a number of San Rimini's business and charitable organizations. In her previous position as United States Ambassador to Uganda, she developed a reputation for effectiveness. We are fortunate to have her in San Rimini and expect that the media will see a great deal of her both in her public role and in social settings, just as they did Ambassador Cartwright."

Zeno made a note to himself. That settled, Eduardo asked Sergio to report on his group meetings regarding the Strada project. As expected, the Grand Prix organizers wanted a firm date for completion before lending their support, as well as a specific list of any proposed changes that could affect the course. The casino owners wanted to know about the availability of government financing due to the increased costs of changing their entrances during construction, should their primary entrances be inaccessible. The transportation minister had a question about routing buses around the area while work was being done, but praised the fact that the proposed changes would make it easier for police, fire, and ambulance services to respond to emergencies throughout the area.

"The Central District Historical Society has provided a substantial list of concerns," Sergio said. "We're working through those point by point. Of all the stakeholders, they will take the longest to bring to consensus. I have experts meeting with them twice this week. I've also started to sow seeds in parliament so they know this is coming and understand that our intent is to submit a plan that has the backing of all the affected groups and a substantial amount of financial and safety research behind it."

Zeno jumped in. "For better or worse, that means the media is now aware of the proposal. A reporter left a message this morning to ask why Sergio met with the casino owners and whether it had to do with roadway construction. Sergio and I will work together on a statement so it's ready for my press briefing. We want the media to convey the need for upgrades and that there is a well-crafted plan in place to protect the area's business interests and its history as improvements are made."

"Good. Once the statement is ready, send me a copy so I have talking points."

Zeno nodded, then ran through several unrelated items for the week's press briefings, including follow-up questions he predicted he would receive about Amanda's due date. Luisa entered to refill the water pitcher and offer more coffee. Margaret Halaby gave reports on several royal charities and relayed a request that King Eduardo become patron of a new organization, one that had been created to identify and assist elderly or disabled citizens who lacked family support. "I drafted a brief with the essential information for your review," she said. "I believe the organization is well structured both in terms of financials and their mission. If you are unable to act as patron, I would recommend either Prince Marco or Princess Isabella."

Eduardo tucked the information into a folder to take to his study while Margaret checked her phone for the final tally from Saturday night's Royal Foundation fundraiser at the opera. Her staff had sent it moments before, which meant Zeno could use the information in his morning briefing and the king would have the figure should anyone inquire.

They were nearly finished when Luisa opened the door. "Your Highness, Teodora Rossi's car just entered the rear gate. She's the new head of the San Riminian Cancer Council. Will you be ready in five minutes?"

"We're wrapping up now."

"Then I'll escort her to the library. I'm told that she is engaged to her longtime partner and is to be married next month."

"Good to know. I'll be there shortly."

Luisa often provided information he could use to relax his guests. Over the years, such tidbits had come in handy. He committed the information to memory and was halfway to the library when his phone vibrated in his pocket. He glanced at the screen and smiled at the number. Conscious of staff in adjacent rooms, he answered with a low, "Hello, Claire?"

"Bad time?"

"I'm walking to a meeting and have exactly three minutes."

"Same, but I'm in the car." He heard the strain in her voice, though she tried to mask it. "I assume you've heard of a tabloid called *Today's Royals?*"

She quickly told him about an article the embassy's Public Affairs Officer had spotted and gave an overview of the morning news reports, which avoided the innuendo of the tabloid. "He's about to watch the daily press briefing from the palace to see what your press secretary says."

"He's going to tell the truth," Eduardo said, then repeated exactly what he'd told Zeno.

"A reputation for effectiveness? I appreciate that."

Eduardo slowed his pace and lowered his voice as he entered the hallway where the library was located. "I'm used to dealing with the media, even with *Today's Royals*, but this is uncharted territory for me."

"Just a moment," she said. He heard her tell her driver to turn onto Via San Vito and stop near the guard station.

"You're going to parliament?" he asked when she came back on the line.

"I have a meeting with Monica Barrata that was moved up from this afternoon. As you were saying?"

"Uncharted territory." He stopped walking. To his right, a row of windows overlooked the palace gardens. Out there, all seemed tranquil. "Claire, I want to keep seeing you."

"I'm beginning to wonder if that's wise."

"You like me."

She laughed at his blunt statement. "That has nothing to do with wisdom."

"Come to La Rocca tonight and we can talk. Miroslav is on duty. I'll send him to your residence to get you. He will be discreet."

Several seconds passed in silence. Eduardo's throat tightened as he waited.

"Claire? Are you there?"

"Yes. Is ten too late? My street is quiet after nine."

Relief washed through him. "Done."

JOHN'S WORDS marinated in the back of Claire's brain all day. During their lunch meeting, they'd brainstormed possible media questions about her night at the opera and drafted a slew of answers. In the end, they'd ditched them all in favor of having John sidestep when he could reasonably do so. Otherwise, he'd answer queries with language similar to what Zeno Amendola had used during the morning press briefing at the palace.

By the time Claire followed Miroslav through the palace corridors and up the staircase that led to King Eduardo's private apartment, past gilt-framed mirrors and portraits of past monarchs, she knew what she had to do.

It tore at her heart, but John had been right when he'd confronted her in the break room. With Eduardo, a relationship needed to be all or nothing, and what were the odds a relationship with Eduardo would be forever? She didn't have a good track record on that front. Her bare ring finger was evidence of that. Besides, there were major obstacles to leap before they could even get to serious, let alone permanent.

And that was if they had enough time to date like normal human beings. She was a true believer in the notion that good relationships were built over time, during moments of laughter and late-night debates. During lazy vacations and shared tasks, during days of sorrow and joy, stress and exhilaration.

Deep down, she knew she and Eduardo had the potential to build that kind of relationship. But she also knew the price they could each pay for a chance at it.

Miroslav knocked on the king's door, then punched a code into the entry pad without waiting for a response. Over his shoulder, he said. "His Highness asked that I let you in when you arrive."

She thanked him, then strode past Miroslav into the vestibule. The king was crossing the great room as she entered. He wore dress slacks, a white shirt, and polished shoes, but his tie was gone and he'd rolled back his sleeves to expose his forearms. The only light came from a lamp beside the sofa. A pair of reading glasses lay there on top of a notebook she guessed contained his daily briefing materials.

One look at him and she wanted to be in his arms.

Before temptation made her do something stupid, she said, "We need to end this. I didn't want to do it on the phone."

Eduardo's eyes widened fractionally and his gaze swept past her. "Thank you, Miroslav, I'm set for the night."

"I'll be available should you need me."

Claire's face heated. She'd thought Miroslav had stayed in the hall. When the door closed, she said, "I'm sorry about that, Your Highness."

It was becoming quite the day for apologies. First with John, then with Eduardo. She probably owed Karen an apology somewhere in there, too.

Eduardo approached slowly, pausing when he was within arm's reach. "Which part?"

"I should have made sure we were alone."

"First, I'm not often alone. Second, I trust Miroslav."

She started to speak, but he continued, "Third, now that we are alone, don't call me Your Highness. I'd much prefer Eduardo. It throws off the balance between us if we're to continue seeing each other. And fourth...you said something else when you walked in. I don't believe I remember what it was."

Claire sighed. He was going to be charming and make this difficult. Having him stand so close was an added difficulty. "You know what I said."

His bright blue eyes filled with both appreciation and concern. "I know what you said. I'd hoped you'd changed your mind in the last thirty seconds."

"You're making it very hard to do this."

"Good. It shouldn't be easy. I don't want to end this."

"We should."

He had the audacity to smile. "Were you hoping to do better than a king? If so, I'm not certain there are many options for you, even as brilliant and gorgeous and intriguing as you are."

"Please be serious. We're courting disaster, Your Highness. The media won't get easier. It's putting the embassy's press office under needless stress."

"It's their job. You didn't embezzle funds or cheat on your taxes, you went on a date. My guess is that they're talented enough at what they do to turn any resulting publicity to the embassy's advantage."

She blew out a hard breath. "I don't like putting them in that position. And it's not as if this is a great situation for you. If I were Sergio or Zeno or any of your other advisors, knowing that your biggest goal over the next few weeks is to introduce important legislation that will face resistance from a number of powerful interests, I'd tell you that the last thing you should be doing is risking your public image. I'm a one-way ticket to a public image problem."

"You're an ambassador. You have a great reputation. I wasn't lying when I said it to Zeno, and he wasn't lying when he said it in this morning's press briefing."

"Did you tell him that we were on a date?"

"Not in so many words, but he understood. Even so, it's not his business."

"The citizens of this country will make it his business. The public feels that their royal families owe them access. If journalists, let alone the tabloids, think there's a story, especially something they can sensationalize, they'll run with whatever they can—"

He reached for her hand and held it. "Claire."

"What? I'm right and you know it."

"You're attracted to me."

She groaned in exasperation. "What does that matter?"

He reached for her other hand, then raised both of them to his chest. "It matters a great deal. I'm attracted to you. You're attracted to me. Neither one of us has been in a relationship in quite a while and there are good reasons for that. Given how long it has taken us to find each other, don't you think we owe it to ourselves to pursue it?"

"It's not that simple."

"I thought that at first, too. But if I weren't a king and you weren't an ambassador, and we were just Eduardo and Claire, we'd be all over each other."

The way he said it made her face heat. "Except part of the attraction is that you're a king and I'm an ambassador. Our jobs have shaped who we are. They've given us a sense of responsibility and the opportunity to see the best and worst in people."

A smug grin lifted his lips. "So you admit it. You *are* attracted to me."

"I thought I made that clear at the opera."

"A man likes to be certain."

"You're not worried about what your staff will think? Or your family? You have four children."

"Grown children, all of whom are in healthy relationships themselves. I imagine they'll adjust. A few months ago, Isabella even asked if I'd consider dating again."

"Asking doesn't mean she's comfortable with it."

"Knowing Isabella, she'd be more than comfortable with it. She'd encourage it."

TO KISS A KING | 137

Claire wanted to warn him of all the other issues they'd face, but he tightened his hold on her hands, distracting her. Gently, he asked, "Do you remember the first song the orchestra played at your credentials ceremony?"

"Yes." Emotion welled within her, tightening her throat. "'Let the Rest of the World Go By.'"

"It's good advice."

"You really need to see that movie."

"We promised each other it would be our next date. In fact, you're the one who made it a condition of the opera date. You seem like the kind of woman who keeps her promises."

She eased her fingers from his, but instead of walking away, she framed his face between her hands. What she saw in his gaze uncoiled the tension she'd carried since the moment she'd seen John Oglethorpe that morning. Everything about the man standing before her spoke to a need in the depths of her soul. His sense of humor, his relentless drive, his heart.

It didn't hurt that he was damned good looking.

She desperately wanted to hold on and let the rest of the world go by.

"That promise was idiocy, Eduardo."

His hands went to her waist and he kissed her, long and slow and sweet. Then he pulled her into a tight hug, lifting her onto her toes as he dropped a kiss near her ear.

"Now you're stuck with me," he said into her hair. "No one gets to call me by my first name unless they're stuck with me."

"You told me to."

"Yes, I did."

He moved to kiss her again. Against his lips, she murmured, "Make it worth my while."

CHAPTER 15

EDUARDO COULDN'T BELIEVE his good fortune.

He held Claire closer as she returned his kiss. He'd been about to lose her. When she'd walked in the door, he had no doubt she'd thought long and hard about the consequences of forging ahead with their relationship. Hearing her say the words *we need to end this* sent his stomach plummeting.

In that same instant, he knew there was nothing he wouldn't do for her. He'd only known her a few weeks, but he'd meant what he'd told her on the catwalk. He was old enough to know his own heart and mind. This—with her—was right.

He wouldn't let her go, not if Claire felt half of what he did. Not if she was ending it out of fear, especially if that fear had nothing to do with what was happening between the two of them and everything to do with people whose opinions didn't matter.

Arguing wouldn't convince her. The woman negotiated for a living. So he fell to his next best weapon: a full out charm assault.

Grazie a Dio, it had worked.

Claire stretched onto her toes, one hand clenching his back while the other went to his hair. Every nerve in his body sizzled to life. It'd been far too long since he'd felt this, but he hadn't wanted it with anyone else.

He wanted it with her.

He wanted to kiss her like this for the rest of the night. He wanted to explore every part of her with his hands and his mouth and his eyes. And he wanted her hands on him, driving him to the edge.

A sigh escaped her as he explored a spot below her jaw. Her fingers grazed his scalp and he heard her sharp intake of breath as her breasts rose against his chest.

The pressure sent shards of desire through him.

"You had a haircut."

Against her collarbone, he said, "That noticeable?"

"The minute I walked in the door. I have a bad habit of noticing everything about you. You're far too handsome for your own good."

The words *take that, Giovanni* ricocheted through his mind, then disappeared as Claire's mouth met his once more. He slid his hand under the back of her blouse, then spread his fingers across the warm skin of her lower back. As their kisses deepened and their hands continued to explore, he eased her toward his bedroom. He paused a few steps from the doorway, savoring the opportunity to look at her where there was light.

She looked different, too. Then he realized what it was and grinned. There were tiny freckles across her nose and cheekbones. "You're not wearing any makeup. I haven't seen you without it."

"I have on mascara."

"Oh."

They looked at each other for a long moment, each keenly aware of the other's breathing, of their bodies pressed to one another, of the heat they shared.

Finally, she said, "I thought it would be easier to end things if I looked bad."

"You don't look bad. You look beautiful." He meant it. She was absolutely stunning.

"That was a failure, then."

He kept his gaze on hers, then slowly freed the top button on her blouse. "You should fail more often. It builds character."

Her lips parted as he worked his way down, slipping each pearly white button through its hole. When the entirety was undone, he slid his hands inside and pressed a long kiss to the top of one breast.

"You lied to me," she whispered. "You said I wouldn't catch fire if I touched you."

He lifted his head but didn't release his grip. His brain clouded with the intensity of the moment. As if intoxicated, he uttered the only word that came to mind. "Stay."

CLAIRE WANTED nothing more than to melt into Eduardo diTalora. The brush of his stubble against her skin as he kissed her throat, the masculine, spicy scent of him, the firm pressure of his hands...all of it made her want to stay with him forever, wrapped in his arms, making love until they couldn't move, then doing it all again. She craved him like she'd never craved another human being in her whole life.

What he was doing with his hand made her so dizzy she could hardly think.

She blew the air from her lungs. "I can't." When he tensed, she clarified, "Not overnight. I have to be at work early and you do, too."

"I've never wanted the option to call in sick. But right now, I wish I could." He pushed her blouse down her shoulders, then his tongue and mouth worked magic on her collarbone.

"A few hours?" she asked.

He answered with a deep, passionate kiss full of promise. She'd told him to make it worth her while. He was. His hands went to her rear and he lifted her, urging her to wrap her legs around him.

"You're okay with—"

"Yes." To emphasize the point, he squeezed her tighter and lifted her, then moved backward until they tumbled as one onto his bed. In the back of her mind, common sense told her to slow down, but she couldn't. She wanted her mouth on his, his body pressing into hers.

She pulled at his shirt, attempting to free it from his slacks. He moved her hand aside and jerked the fabric, then unfastened the buttons and tossed the shirt away without removing his mouth from hers. They both went for the hem of his undershirt at the same time. A moment later, it joined his shirt on the floor.

He had far more muscle than she would have guessed, even knowing how often he ran or saw a trainer. She reveled in exploring it all. His hands forked into her hair as she dragged her mouth along his chest. He toed off his shoes and she heard two quick thumps as they hit the floor.

She spread her hands across the planes of his abdomen, wondering at the dedication it took to stay so fit.

Then her lips found the scar. In the dark of his room, she couldn't see it, but she moved her fingers to where her mouth had been and traced its raised edge.

"I'm perfectly fine," he whispered.

"This was serious surgery."

"*Was.*" His hand covered hers. "They repaired the defect and I'm better now than I was before. Every millimeter of my heart has been mapped and studied. I have a lot of life left in me. I want to live it."

She dropped a kiss to the scar and lingered there, imagining how vulnerable Eduardo must have felt in the days and weeks before undergoing the operation. Given how many people admired him and relied on him, he couldn't have shown his apprehension, even as he faced the enormous risk of putting his life in someone else's hands.

His hands went to her hips and he eased her along his body so they were chest to chest, forehead to forehead. He gave her a soft, romantic kiss, then smoothed her hair from her face. "*Bella donna,* make love to me."

"It's been a while since I've done this."

"Good."

"Good? That's your response?"

"It means I might stand a chance of fooling you if you have certain expectations of my skills based on my title."

"I could say the same. You know…making love to an ambassador."

His hands went to her backside. "One who still has her pants and shoes on."

"Then do something about it."

The words were hardly out before he rolled her to her back and did exactly as she asked. He took more time with her bra and panties, his tongue and fingers making a slow discovery of each curve until she had her legs anchored around his hips. Then, on an agonizing breath, he was inside her. He held her hands, fingers interlaced, as they moved together. At first, they each went slowly, adjusting to each other, taking stock of the moment. As tension built between them and their skin grew more heated, they found their flow. Claire's breath started to come in gasps and her eyes drifted closed as she whispered Eduardo's name.

Whatever her expectations might have been, this went beyond any of them. Beyond her imagination.

He murmured something indistinguishable in Italian near her ear, then shifted and changed the rhythm. As her body yearned for more and more, he caught her earlobe between his teeth. She arched into him even as her mind spiraled in ecstasy. His pace quickened as he drove into her. Moments later, his fingers clenched around hers and he groaned against her temple.

She couldn't get enough of him.

After a long, deep kiss, he guided her to her side so he could drop his head beside hers on the pillow. They held each other for a long time, their breath mingling, their skin slowly cooling, as he caressed her hip in languid strokes.

Eventually, he pulled the covers over them for warmth. She shifted so she lay on top of him, her hands folded on his chest and her cheek resting against the back of her hands.

"I think this is the most comfortable bed I've ever been in."

His low laugh rumbled through her palms as he stroked her back, gently at first, then with more pressure.

Then his hands moved lower and she felt him slowly coming to life.

"What were you saying about expectations?" she asked.

"I have no idea. Whatever they may have been...well." He exhaled, then pulled her higher to kiss her on the mouth. "I think we're just fine."

CLAIRE WAS NEARLY asleep and fighting it. She needed to leave, but wanted a few more minutes of indulgence.

They'd made love a second time, after which Eduardo had tucked her head against his shoulder and said, "Can we agree to keep seeing each other after this? If we have that baseline understanding—that we're together in this—we can negotiate how to handle outside variables."

She'd smiled into the crook of his neck, then traced a path down his arm with her fingertips. "I can agree to that."

Saying the words gave her a sense of calm she hadn't felt in a long time. Whatever the coming days brought, she and Eduardo would face it as one.

She sighed against his chest, then let her fingers drift along his side. She loved the feel of his skin, the dips and curves of muscle, the way he reacted to her touch. But she knew further exploration would have to wait.

A phone rang near their heads, shocking them both. Eduardo uttered a curse, then rolled to reach in the direction of his nightstand. "Only the palace switchboard connects to this line."

"It's all right."

She planted a kiss on the back of his neck while he grabbed the receiver and put it to his ear. She slipped from the bed and padded across the floor, searching for her clothes in the darkened room. Eduardo said a few quick words in Italian, but mostly listened. She was partially dressed when he hung up.

"You must have heard the other end of that."

She paused while zipping her pants. "No. Why?"

She could just make him out in the faint light cast from the great room. He swept a hand to encompass her. "You're getting dressed."

She sat near his feet and shook out her blouse, trying to determine which way was right side out. "I was debating how long I could stay without falling asleep when the phone rang. Mine is somewhere in the other room...what happened? Is there a crisis of some sort?"

"No. Not that kind of crisis." She finished buttoning her blouse and he kicked his feet over the side of the bed so he sat beside her. He smoothed her hair away from her face. "There are reporters camped out at the front and back entrances. Sergio and Zeno are on their way. Apparently someone saw you and Miroslav enter the building and tipped off the press."

Claire felt herself blanch.

"It's all right," he assured her. "I told them to give us ten minutes. I'll get dressed and we'll take you back to your residence. We have corridors that very few staff members know of, though I'm confident it wasn't the staff who leaked the information. Nick and Isabella hosted a reception in the garden earlier. Any of the guests walking along the paths could have seen you in the car with Miroslav when you entered the rear gate."

"That's possible," she admitted. She'd also noted a long line of dark cars parked along the Strada il Reggiménto, which ran adjacent to the palace. Drivers lingered between the vehicles, chatting and smoking cigarettes. One of them could have recognized her as they awaited their clients' departure from the palace. Either way, she'd been foolish to lean forward in her seat for a look at the palace as she and Miroslav had approached.

"Miroslav or one of the other security team members will get you home safely," Eduardo promised. "Sergio and Zeno will troubleshoot if there's a problem."

Eduardo dressed as she wiggled into her shoes. They were both in the great room, seated on one of its large sofas, when a knock came at the door, then Miroslav entered with Sergio, Zeno, and Luisa at his heels.

Eduardo looked at his assistant in surprise. "Luisa, you didn't need to come in."

"I saw the reporters' vans go by my flat and called the security office to see what was happening. I thought you could use my assistance."

"She drove her Renault," Miroslav told Eduardo. "It will draw less attention than taking one of the palace cars. The banquet crew is about to leave, so Luisa can take the ambassador at the same time."

"Thank you, Luisa, that's very generous." Claire said.

"I'm happy to do it, Madam Ambassador."

Claire looked to Miroslav. "Will I need to duck down in the back?"

Eduardo put a hand on her knee, drawing her attention. "You don't have to hide if you don't want to. It's up to you. Whether you're seen tonight or not, you'll be seen with me in the future. The palace won't comment other than to say 'we have never commented on the king's private life.'"

Zeno shifted his weight uncomfortably. "I doubt that will work, Your Highness."

"Make it work. Aside from stating that we have deep respect for the ambassador, we have no comment."

He turned to Claire. "I have to go to Denmark on Wednesday. I'll be back late Thursday. Are you free that night?"

Luisa cleared her throat. "Your Highness, you're hosting members of the International Paralympic Committee and a group of San Rimini's Paralympians that evening."

"Friday?"

"You are free on Friday after eight."

Claire smiled. "I'll double check, but I believe I'm free Friday night."

"Movie at my place."

"Do you have popcorn?"

"If not, I believe I have the resources to get some."

"Done."

CHAPTER 16

IN THE FOUR weeks following Claire's nighttime visit to La Rocca and her fabulously unsuccessful attempt to end their relationship, they had made four unsuccessful attempts to see *Out of Africa.*

After attempts two, three, and four, Eduardo felt compelled to point out that the first failure was Claire's fault.

Their original date, on the Friday night after they'd first made love, was rescheduled when a prominent American businessman was arrested and Claire was compelled to stay late at the office. Movie dates two and three were canceled when Eduardo had dinners run longer than expected, though they managed to meet for shorter dates at both the palace and at her residence. They'd taken care to avoid the media, and their efforts kept speculation about their relationship on the back burner, buried at the end of reports. It had helped that Aletta's sister, Helena Masciaretti, was photographed walking hand-in-hand with a well-known Scottish actor ten years her junior, drawing the attention of both royal watchers and the tabloid press.

For once, Eduardo was more than happy to have Helena in the limelight.

The fourth movie night was scrapped when Arturo and Paolo, Prince Federico's sons, both came down with strep throat. Before being diagnosed, they'd spent the afternoon in Eduardo's apartment curled up on his sofa watching television, and he wanted a day to ensure the room was cleaned and that no one else in the family was ill.

The fifth attempt was arranged for a Saturday at the palace.

"We won't be interrupted this time," Eduardo promised Claire over dinner at Trattoria Safina, an inconspicuous restaurant located on the Via Vespri, a block downhill from the Strada il Teatro. They'd arrived late on a Friday night, after most tourists had left the area for their hotels and only a few locals remained. Two journalists had spotted Claire entering the restaurant and were staked out across the street, but the trattoria's shades were positioned such that the men couldn't identify her dinner companion. Otherwise, Claire and Eduardo had peace and quiet. Basia, the young woman who worked the front of the trattoria, kept an eagle eye on the street. She was the type who could scare off a professional bodybuilder with a glare, despite her small size and wildly colored hair.

Over mushroom-stuffed ravioli and fresh bread dipped in herbed olive oil, they talked about work, then family. Eduardo's grandsons had recovered from strep and had been running around the palace garden that afternoon.

"Tomorrow night, we can have an early dinner at La Rocca," Eduardo said. "If it's all right with you, Amanda and Marco could join us. I know you met them at the credentials ceremony, but I want them to get to know you. They wouldn't stay late, so we could watch the movie afterward."

Claire took a long, tantalizing sip of her wine and eyed him over the rim of her glass. When she finally set it down, she said, "Spending time with Amanda and Marco would be wonderful, but I have to warn you: I won't want popcorn after dinner. Movies require popcorn."

"Are you canceling already? Over popcorn?" He gave her a withering look, but she laughed it off.

"No. But don't expect me to eat a lot at dinner, even with Samuel doing the cooking. Not eating one of his meals is going to take an enormous amount of willpower. I want that sacrifice recognized and rewarded."

"So noted." He made a face. "But I won't do it in front of Samuel."

"You don't know how good you have it with him."

"I do know. But if I admit it to him, he'll double down on the oatmeal. I'm not sure I can survive that."

She grinned and told him to enjoy his ravioli.

THE NEXT EVENING, Fabiano dropped Claire at La Rocca just as Marco and Amanda passed the rear entrance. Though she'd met Amanda the night she'd presented her credentials and had the chance to greet Prince Marco briefly that night, she hadn't seen the couple since. Claire wasn't sure what to expect, particularly from Prince Marco, but both greeted her warmly. Together, they climbed the stairs to King Eduardo's apartment. Marco tapped in the code at the keypad. As they entered the vestibule, they heard voices coming from the great room.

They entered to see Samuel Barden standing beside the king at the table. Both men had their backs to the door. Samuel had one hand on his hip as he gestured toward a low floral centerpiece and said something about using an arrangement from the family dining room instead.

"Not romantic enough," Eduardo replied. "Not if it's the orange and yellow arrangement that was there during breakfast this morning."

Amanda, Marco, and Claire exchanged looks.

"Do you have anything pink? I think Claire likes pink."

"I do like pink," she said as she moved toward them, surprising both Eduardo and Samuel. "But what's on the table already is beautiful. Let's leave it." To Samuel, she said, "Thank you. This is lovely, as always."

Eduardo gave the table a long look, but his disappointment was apparent.

Samuel said, "Dinner will be ready in a half hour, if that's suitable. I've left wine and sparkling water on the bar."

Once he was gone, Marco and Amanda went for drinks and Claire gave Eduardo a gentle kiss on the cheek. Near his ear, she murmured, "Not romantic enough? That's very sweet."

"We've tried to have movie night for weeks now. I wanted to get it right."

"We're both here. That's all we need."

For the next two hours, they enjoyed a delicious dinner and conversation. At one point, Eduardo crossed the room to retrieve a bowl from the bar. When he set it in front of Claire, she laughed so hard she could hardly speak.

"Banduzzi olives," Eduardo announced.

"And this is funny…how?" Amanda asked.

"At our first dinner here in the residence—a business dinner, I must add—I had Samuel leave some on the bar so Claire could try them. I'd sent a Banduzzi olive tree to the embassy as a welcome gift with the dinner invitation and promised to serve them."

Marco eyed his father. "What happened?"

"It was all I could do not to stare at her once she entered the residence. I managed to mix decent Negronis and talk to Claire somewhat intelligently about policy initiatives, but I completely forgot the olives."

"You distracted him," Amanda said. "That's rare."

The smile Marco gave his father made Claire feel welcomed all over again.

They'd just finished dessert when Amanda mentioned to Claire that her father, a former ambassador to Italy, had followed Claire's career. "He teaches a course each spring at American University, so he keeps up on a lot of the initiatives at embassies around the world. He told me he was very impressed with some of the programs you worked on during your time in Uganda."

Claire expected Amanda to mention the education program, but instead, it was a maternal health care program that had caught her interest. "I knew there can be a lack of access to maternity care, but I had no idea about the incidence of obstetric fistulas. It's horrifying to know that so many women—teenagers, even—end up with such devastating injuries from labor, then are left to fend for themselves."

Claire nodded. "Horrifying is the perfect descriptor for it. Thankfully, there are some wonderful organizations working in Uganda to educate people about the problem and the need for preventive care. They're also recruiting doctors to perform low- or no-cost surgery so women who've been affected can lead more normal lives. Their work gives me hope."

To Eduardo, she explained, "Our role at the embassy was to facilitate the recruitment of health care educators and surgeons from the United States."

He hadn't heard of the problem, but Amanda said she'd done some reading after speaking with her father. "There are several San Riminian health care workers who've volunteered their time and expertise. Some in Uganda, others in Burkina Faso and Kenya."

Eduardo leaned back in his seat and considered his daughter-in-law with admiration. Claire sensed they'd built a solid respect for each other in the years since Amanda had met and married Marco. "We should be doing more to support them. Once the Strada il Teatro project is done, would you remind me of this conversation?"

"I might be a little busy with my own baby, but I'll make a note. If I don't remind you, perhaps Claire will?"

It didn't escape Claire that Amanda's suggestion assumed that Claire would be around for the long haul. She nodded and said, "I can do that. I met with several fistula patients at a clinic my first year in Uganda. It's not an experience I'll ever forget."

A short time later, they'd adjourned to the sofas and Claire mentioned that she'd had the opportunity to meet Giovanni Sozzani, the king's close friend, when he'd hosted them for lunch two weeks earlier.

"Did he try to convert you to the dark side?" Marco asked.

At Claire's frown, Amanda said, "That's what the king calls cycling. He's a runner, Giovanni is a dedicated cyclist. They debate the merits of one over the other all the time."

"We did discuss cycling," Claire said. "The town where I grew up draws a lot of cyclists in the summer. We talked about New Mexico and Colorado and the cycling events held there. But he didn't try to convert me."

"I warned him," Eduardo said. "She refuses to run. I can't fathom it, but I can live with it. If Claire were to start cycling, though, I'm not sure how I'd handle it."

"I told him that taking a spin class doesn't count as cycling," Claire noted. "But I prefer hiking when I can, anyway."

Amanda agreed and said she and Marco had been trying to schedule extra hiking time on their weekends so she could keep moving throughout her pregnancy. "Having that outdoor time is the only thing that keeps me from being exhausted. It refills the energy well."

"And that," Marco said, "is our cue to leave. It's getting late, and my wife and baby need to sleep."

"The baby can sleep whether or not I sleep."

Marco shrugged and stood, but the stealthy wink he shot at Amanda made it obvious he simply wanted his wife alone.

Once they were gone, Eduardo asked Claire if she was still awake enough for the movie.

"For that particular movie? Always."

Eduardo strode toward the coffee table in search of the remote control. "He likes you, you know."

"Who? Marco?"

"Yes." Eduardo located the remote, then smiled at her. "He was very close to his mother and has always been protective of her legacy. But not only does he like you, he likes me with you. He told me that last part this morning when we finalized the time for dinner. He said I've been at my best recently."

Claire felt tears come to her eyes. She still remembered watching the late queen's funeral on television. The pained looks on her family's faces had spoken volumes, Marco's expression in particular. She smiled at Eduardo through the wave of emotion that suddenly gripped her. "Thank you for telling me."

"I thought you should know." He gave her a long, heartfelt smile, then turned toward the far wall and pushed a button on the remote to reveal a television that was hidden behind a painting. As the painting slid to the side, he admitted, "I don't have the opportunity to watch television that often. Arturo and Paolo assured me that I can get the movie on here and showed me how to find it in the menu."

Claire moved behind Eduardo and wrapped her arms around his waist as he hit the power button. "I love that your grandchildren teach you things about your own apartment."

"They're too smart for their own good. Federico has to work hard to keep up with them."

Claire planted a kiss on the back of Eduardo's neck, then offered to refill his water glass. As she moved to the bar, she said, "I know what I said earlier about popcorn, but I can watch without it. Dinner was far too tempting for me to save room."

Eduardo made a sound of agreement, but didn't speak. When she turned from the bar, water glasses in hand, his eyes were riveted on the television. He raised his hand and clicked the remote to change the channel, but not before Claire saw her own face on the screen and heard the reporter use the phrase, "her past."

"Go back."

He glanced at her with concern in his eyes, then hit a button. The screen showed an old, blurry photo of Claire with her ex-husband.

"Oh, for crying out loud," she muttered. "This is ancient history. He's all they could dig up about me? Next thing you know, they'll pull out my seventh-grade school picture. I had a painfully uneven haircut for that one."

"You know how these go," Eduardo said. "They don't have anything newsworthy to run, so they go searching for old information they can make sound new and intriguing."

"I suppose."

For over a month, she and Eduardo had stayed the course with the media. They'd agreed to remain silent for the time being and to continue leading their lives, deciding it was the only way they could enjoy their time together and truly get to know each other.

Helena Masciaretti's new, high-profile relationship had given them the breathing room necessary to accomplish that. There had been shots of Claire entering and leaving La Rocca, and even a few of them strolling through the palace garden that had been taken with a long lens by someone who'd climbed on top of a bus shelter on the Strada il Reggiménto. In each instance, Zeno Amendola and John Oglethorpe had told reporters they had no comment about their bosses' personal lives. With little to use, the press had—for the most part—run with other stories.

This report, however, felt different, even as the announcer noted that Claire had been married for two years in her early twenties. Her voice promised scandal.

Then she delivered. A photo of her ex that looked current filled the screen. In a voiceover that had sounded prerecorded, the announcer said, "This is David Arnold Smith today." The shot panned out to reveal that he was holding a board under his face with his name on it.

A curse went through Claire's mind as the announcer continued, "Last night, Smith was booked into the Santa Clara County Jail in San Jose, California, for public intoxication after leaving a strip club. A friend spoke to one of our reporters about the incident on the condition of anonymity. That friend told us that Smith is not a regular at the strip club, but went there because he and his friends were unable to visit their usual bar."

The shot cut to the back of a man's head, partially blurred, as he spoke to a reporter in a parking lot. Behind the reporter, the bottom edge of a flashing neon sign was visible. "Yeah, David's a good guy. Good guy. He's like, being stalked because of his ex-wife. It's just wrong, ya know? The guy can't even go out with his friends and get a drink without being harassed, all 'cause of a woman who cheated on him. He's got a new wife and he has moved on."

The last two words were louder and slurred.

The screen returned to the booking photo and the original announcer continued, "David Arnold Smith has had a number of run-ins with the law over the years, all for public intoxication. However, his last arrest was nearly five years ago. He is said to blame Claire Peyton for this latest incident. We have reached out to the ambassador's office for comment, but they have not responded to our request."

"I expect my phone will ring any minute." Claire put a hand to her forehead. "This is asinine. I haven't seen him in well over twenty years. I had no idea he was in California. And I most certainly did *not* cheat on him."

Eduardo muted the television, then wrapped an arm around her waist and eased her to his side. "I'm sorry, Claire."

"That was an American network, wasn't it? That means my parents will see it. That's the last thing they need. He was atrocious to them."

"With any luck, they'll tune it out. They know the truth about you."

She cast a sideways look at him. "You believe me."

"Don't doubt it for a moment."

"Thank you."

He set the remote on the coffee table and urged her to take a seat beside him on the sofa. "Would you care to give me the nutshell version of the story? I'd tell you about my marriage, but there have been books written on it. If you aren't sick of hearing about it, you should be."

She laughed at that. He had a way of putting her at ease, even under less-than-ideal circumstances. "The nutshell version is that marrying David was a huge mistake. We met in college. He flirted, sent flowers, said all the right things. He loved that I worked hard and had ambition, because he did, too, at least at first. But we didn't know each other well enough to be married. I knew he liked to go to bars with the guys on the weekends to watch sports, but I had no clue how much he drank or that it was more than just the weekends. Not until we were married and moved in together. I kept finding empty bottles in the bottom of our trash bins and jammed beneath the seats of his car. I worked long hours and he was doing well at his job, which made it easier to hide his addiction. When I confronted him, he lied about it. Then he insisted it wasn't a problem and that I was being a killjoy. Gave me a whole spiel about how he needed an outlet from a stressful job and that he was simply getting adjusted to working full time and being married."

Claire took a deep breath. She hated digging up the past, but she didn't want it to affect her future. "Anyway, I told him it was over unless he got help, so he agreed. One afternoon I picked up a gas receipt he'd dropped in our carport. It was for a station on the far side of town and was time-stamped for when he'd told me he was at therapy. That's how I discovered he was sleeping with an ex-girlfriend. Her apartment complex was across the street from that gas station. He confessed to it when I handed him the receipt and told me it wouldn't have happened if I hadn't been such a nag about a drinking problem he didn't have. I moved out the next morning and filed for divorce as soon as I could find an attorney. We were legally married for two years, but only lived together for six months."

Eduardo shook his head. He didn't need to say anything. Claire knew from his expression that he understood how stressful that phase of her life had been and that he wasn't judging her for it.

"What did he do to your parents?"

"He called them continuously starting the day I moved out. Told them I had taken money from him and that they should do the honorable thing and repay him. I hadn't, of course, and they knew it. They quit answering the phone, so he sent a friend to their home in New Mexico to ask for money. The guy went away when they refused, but having someone show up on their doorstep scared them. I got a restraining order against David and my parents did the same. Thankfully, he gave up and we never heard from him again. He didn't even show up for the divorce hearing." She folded one leg under her and turned on the sofa so she faced Eduardo. "I felt guilty for quite a while afterward. I hated that my lapse in judgment caused grief for my parents. And deep down, I'd always thought of marriage as forever. I knew I'd made the right decision to leave, but it still felt like a personal failure. On the other hand, the experience made me both more cautious and more perceptive. Eventually, I decided that if my worst mistake in life was a poor marriage that I got out of relatively unscathed, I was doing all right."

He put a hand on her knee. "The story will blow over. If you had been married to him recently or he came off as credible, it'd be different. It's obvious that he's made foolish choices and is looking for someone to blame. Your profile makes you an easy target."

"And you. That's what worries me."

"I'm fine. I've endured far worse." He gave her knee a squeeze, then slid his hand higher before leaning in for a kiss. "Since your phone is quiet, I'll assume that your staff thinks that you're fine, too. Let's watch a movie. If anything comes of the report, we'll weather it together."

She sighed. "You know that this won't be the last. Stories will come up. A former embassy employee from one of my early postings will say I was rude to them at a dinner. A citizen who had a problem getting a visa will tell a reporter I was incompetent and caused them to lose business. Some of it may even be true."

"You aren't incompetent."

"You know what I mean, Eduardo. Every little thing, even events I can't recall, can be weaponized."

"I'd say that it's a good thing you have a knight in shining armor to defend you, but you're far from a damsel in distress. Instead, I'll simply say that you can trust me to listen to you and to have your back when you need me."

"You know, you make a fine diplomat."

"High compliment coming from you."

She gave him a kiss, then said, "Let's watch a movie."

CHAPTER 17

EDUARDO WAS STILL SCROLLING through the television menu when Claire's phone rang. They'd spent a solid ten minutes trying to find *Out of Africa*, but the search function kept locking up and he'd had to start over.

She glanced at her phone. "It's the embassy."

"You can use my private study."

"No, it'll be John Oglethorpe. I'll keep it brief." She gestured toward the screen. "You live in a palace with access to a million channels. The movie has to be available somewhere. It won Best Picture."

He continued searching while Claire answered. Even from an arm's length away, he could hear the voice on the other end say, "Madam Ambassador, I have the President on the line. Would you hold, please?"

Claire stiffened. Eduardo gestured toward his study. She went, but didn't close the door. He continued reading the endless list of available movies, but he could hear enough of the conversation to know that Claire was playing defense. Yes, she'd seen the report. She hadn't seen David Smith in over twenty years, and that information was covered in her SF-86, which Eduardo took to be some type of security or background form. Then she was quiet for a moment. There was a, "Yes, Mr.

President," and a few words of thanks. A moment later, Claire said, "No, it isn't a concern. If he were a member of parliament, that would be different, but in this case, there are far fewer areas where a conflict could arise. In those cases, I'm cognizant of the issues, as is he." Another pause, and then, in a more positive tone, "There's been good progress. I've locked up two and have a third on the hook. It's just a matter of reeling him to shore. I have a phone call scheduled with the fourth on Wednesday. She'll be the toughest, but I have a good staff and they've prepared persuasive arguments. I'm confident I can arrange a face to face meeting." Another pause. Then Claire said, "I value it, as well. Thank you, Mr. President. I'll keep you updated. Enjoy the rest of your weekend."

Claire stepped back into the room, then sagged against the wall beside the entrance to his study.

"Sounded pleasant," Eduardo said, allowing the sarcasm to show on his face.

Claire laughed. "It could have been a lot worse."

"About David Smith?"

"That's what prompted it. But it sounds like he's had me on his radar for a while. David gave him an excuse to check in."

"Because of me?"

Claire gave a noncommittal shrug. "He hasn't been in office long. The last thing he wants is any hint of scandal. I assured him we are being careful to avoid anything that can be construed as a conflict of interest. For the time being, I think I've allayed his concerns. It helped that we each had good news about the education initiative."

That was the part of the call that had piqued Eduardo's curiosity. "Do tell."

She eased off the wall and nodded as she approached the sofa. "He spoke with the new ambassador in Uganda yesterday. Poland will offer financial support and teachers to the program. Latvia looks like it will come through with a similar commitment. I told him I have a good shot at convincing San Rimini. That let me end the call on a positive note."

"You really think you'll line up the support?"

She gestured for the remote. "Give me that. I'll search."

As she changed screens, she said, "I have Barrata and Galli for certain. Luciano Festa is wavering, but Mark Rosenburg is meeting with him this week. Mark's good. He'll convince Festa."

"And Selvaggi?"

"Still working on her. On the other hand, do you know Ana Maria Marotti?"

"I know the name, but haven't met her. She's new to parliament."

"Mark recommended we get her support, too. She's young and has a degree in education. Marotti is on board. When you introduce that legislation, she's the ideal person to speak to the generation of teachers we most want involved."

"You're that confident you'll get Selvaggi?"

She grinned and leaned into him. "Let's say that I'm optimistic. However, I have a real gripe about your movie selections. Look at this."

A movie poster showing Meryl Streep and Robert Redford sitting on a grassy hill occupied the left side of the screen. On the right was a notation that the film was unavailable at this time.

"So much for being an all-powerful king," she teased.

"Never said I was all powerful. You're confusing me with *The Wizard of Oz*."

"You're a hell of a lot sexier than the Wizard."

"I should hope so." He snuggled her closer, then pressed a kiss to her head. The thought *there's no place like home* fluttered through his brain. Claire made him feel at home.

"Want to watch it?" she asked, raising the remote and scrolling until she found *The Wizard of Oz*. "I haven't seen it in years. We'll get *Out of Africa* another way. Soon."

He held her tighter and said, "Follow the yellow brick road."

ON MONDAY MORNING, Luisa waited at the bottom of the stairs as usual. And, as usual, she handed Eduardo his schedule for the week as they walked from the residential wing to his office.

Before she could inquire about his morning workout, he said, "I have a question for you, Luisa."

She raised a brow.

"Why is it that I can't get *Out of Africa* on the television in my apartment? Is there someone you can call?"

"I'll check and get back to you, Your Highness. I'm sure there's a way to do it. I believe it won Best Picture."

"It did, and I would appreciate that. Now, in answer to the question I know you are dying to ask, today was all about sprints."

Luisa's expression turned to one of astonishment. "She had you run? You should be in a good mood, then."

"Not at all. You see, I'm all about endurance. The long haul. Short and explosive has never suited me. I'd much rather run at a steady pace for an hour than do a twenty-minute series of all-out sprints."

They passed a series of windows that looked onto the garden. Princess Isabella sat on a large blanket on the ground, her legs tucked beneath her as she read to a group of preschool-aged children. A gaggle of parents wielding their phones stood in a semicircle behind the children and took photos. A reporter and photographer were off to the side, covering the event in a more understated fashion than the excited adults.

Isabella sensed movement behind the windows and paused in her reading, then pointed out the king to the children. The parents' phones went upward as if on marionette strings as the children waved. Eduardo waved back, then continued walking with Luisa. As one, the adults' phones swung to their previous positions.

"Princess Isabella is hosting a fairy tale story hour for participants in an early education program," Luisa explained. "She has another session this afternoon, then two scheduled for tomorrow with groups from other schools."

"Nick is working on a research project about the medieval origins of fairy tales. He plans to teach a course on the subject next semester."

"He'll still teach his medieval art course, won't he? I have a niece at the University of San Rimini who is hoping to take it."

"I believe so. The course does fill, though, so if you'd like me to put in a word—"

"Oh, no," Luisa said, waving off the favor. "She told me that Professor Black is good at getting students into his classes off the waitlist as long as they attend the first week or two of class. Now, as to Greta and the sprints—"

"You were supposed to forget that topic."

"When do I forget anything? As to Greta and the sprints, my guess is that she's testing your aerobic capacity versus your anaerobic capacity. It's good to have a balance. Sprints require more muscle."

Eduardo cast a suspicious look at his assistant. "She told you to say that."

"Not in those exact words."

"I feel plotted against. Monarchs develop a sixth sense for that. You should tread carefully."

Luisa merely shrugged. "Think of it as a metaphor for your duties. As a king, your position is one that requires endurance above all else. You're in it for the long haul, but the ability to sprint now and then serves you well."

"Did Greta tell you that, too, hoping I'd embrace sprint work?"

"Oh, no. That was all mine."

"The next time I'm forced to suffer through sprints, I'll be sure to keep it in mind." As they approached the office, he said, "I may need an entire pot of coffee this morning."

"I'll be quick with the refills, then."

He began the meeting as soon as Luisa returned with his coffee. Sergio started with a report on a new parliamentary initiative to shore up the San Rimini Emergency Trust, a fund instituted to help in times of natural disasters. The measure was overdue, so Eduardo was glad to hear it was moving forward. Sergio promised to include the details in the king's briefing book so he could read about it after the meeting.

After that, Sergio flipped to a new page of notes. "Now for the not-so-good news. The staff teams working on the Strada il Teatro project are meeting increased resistance from the casino owners and the Grand Prix organizers. Both groups know we're on a tight timeline and they're trying to work that to their advantage. However, the bigger issue is the drop in your favorability numbers. We have every other group in line, even the Central District Historical Society. But if your numbers go any lower, everyone is going to think they have room to renegotiate."

"What are the latest poll numbers?"

"You've dropped from a high of seventy-seven percent to around sixty-one. That's still a very good number, Your Highness, but the trajectory is concerning."

Eduardo felt the shift in the room, though his senior staff were all careful not to show it.

"What else? Give it to me straight."

"*San Rimini Today* did a piece on Claire Peyton early last week. The usual biographical information, a bit about her time in Uganda, and a description of the work she's done since arriving in San Rimini. It was mostly favorable and had a sidebar about a medical research exchange that took place recently between San Rimini and the United States. However, when a television network did street interviews asking citizens what they thought of the article, most hadn't read it. Instead, they were quick to offer opinions on whether or not you should be dating her. A few wondered whether there could be a conflict of interest, but most said that they couldn't imagine anyone taking Aletta's place. Those interviews were shown repeatedly on Wednesday. That spurred a Thursday morning talk show on a different network into an hour-long discussion on whether Claire should be made a queen if you were to marry."

Sergio gave one of his eyes a brisk rub as he spoke, as if trying to wipe away an exhausting weekend. "Our latest poll was taken on the same Wednesday that the street interviews were broadcast, and the numbers didn't reflect whether the respondent had seen the coverage because the pollsters didn't know to ask. However, the talk show hadn't yet aired, nor had the weekend story about the ambassador's ex-husband. I assume you saw it?"

"I did."

"That could also change the numbers."

Eduardo appreciated that Sergio was careful not to say that his popularity would take another hit, though they all knew it.

"I can handle all of this in the briefing room today," Zeno said. "The story on Claire's ex-husband shouldn't get much traction. He's not credible and that's obvious even to frequent tabloid readers. The rest I'll dismiss just as I do other speculation about your private life."

Sergio nodded along as Zeno spoke, then said, "On the bright side, we have less than a month before we hand off the plan to parliament. There's only so much that can affect your numbers in that time."

"You're saying that it's a race to the finish."

Sergio gave a tilt of the head. "The goal is to maintain. If that can be done, we're fine. Parliament will leap on a plan that has unified support and is backed by a monarch with sixty-one percent favorability. They want this deal done, too, but can't take a personal risk if they're facing election. We're making it as easy as possible for them with minimal political fallout."

On a deep breath, he added, "Thankfully, we don't have to worry about the deal you made with the ambassador. I understand that she has Barrata and Galli on board, but she's still working on Festa. To our knowledge, she hasn't even met with Selvaggi. If she doesn't have Selvaggi, you're under no obligation to introduce her education plan. Keeping our focus on the Strada sends a strong message about your priorities to everyone involved."

Eduardo remained silent. He wasn't going to tell Sergio about Festa, or about the fact that Claire had a phone call scheduled with Selvaggi. The information had been shared in private. Besides, Sergio was right. As long as Claire didn't have Selvaggi on board before the Strada proposal went to parliament, they wouldn't have to deal with it.

Luisa entered to top off everyone's coffee as Sergio wrapped up, then Zeno asked about a few unrelated issues for the morning press briefing. Margaret had reports on work Prince Antony and his wife had completed for the San Riminian Scholarship fund and a follow-up on Eduardo's Our Place appearance several weeks earlier, then she handed him materials she'd prepared for an upcoming event to support research projects at Royal Memorial Hospital.

He thanked her and slid the papers into his briefing binder. As if on cue, Sergio sucked in his lower lip and Zeno looked at the floor.

"I hate to ask, given the expressions on your faces, but is there anything else before we wrap?"

Margaret's face split into a grin, but it was Zeno who cleared his throat. "Yes, Your Highness. I am afraid we have a Code Orange."

Sergio turned away, trying to contain his laughter. Code Orange was their office term for occasions when they were forced to deal with human imperfection and the resulting media spin. The most memorable had occurred during Marco and Amanda's wedding. Federico's sons were caught on live television chewing gum in the pews when gum was famously forbidden in the centuries-old Duomo. When the grinning boys spit the gum into their palms, traded, then popped the wads back into their mouths, the nation's collective gasp of amused revulsion was nearly audible.

Comedians around the world had a field day on their late-night shows. Even serious news programs aired the scene in the final minutes of their broadcasts, claiming it was, "a moment to lighten your day."

Code Orange situations were often ridiculous, but needed to be addressed, lest their coverage detract from the business of state. In the case of the boys, Zeno told the exuberant palace press corps that all parents experienced such indignities with their children and that the boys were now keenly aware of the importance of protecting historical sites.

"What about, ah, sanitary habits?" one bold reporter had asked.

Zeno had pulled off a credible look of lightheartedness, despite feeling anything but. "I imagine they'll be shown that footage at regular intervals for the rest of their lives and it will be every bit as agonizing as being forced to watch ourselves at that age. There are experiences no one wants to relive, particularly on film."

No one uttered the phrase "Code Orange" outside Eduardo's office, lest anyone ask the definition. If it became known that the monarch had a code word for addressing his family's very human foibles, it would—ironically enough—result in yet another Code Orange.

"I suppose we're due. Margaret's still smiling, so it can't be that bad."

Zeno opened his mouth to speak, paused, then started again. "Before she married Prince Marco, Amanda made regular purchases from a major online retailer, one that offered overnight delivery to her college residence hall and to her flat in Washington, D.C."

"I can guess which one. I can also guess what happened. Her purchase history was leaked and one or more items are causing a stir?"

Margaret glanced at Zeno, and Sergio glanced at Margaret. Then they all looked at the king.

"Not quite, Your Highness," Zeno said. "The items were innocuous. Gym shoes, light bulbs, a coffee maker. A lot of books. She left reviews for many of her purchases. They were posted under a screen name, but that name has been definitively linked to your daughter-in-law and the reviews are being republished in multiple outlets."

Eduardo wasn't sure whether to be horrified or to laugh. Amanda was circumspect. Before marrying Marco, she'd served as an etiquette coach to children of diplomats and other high-ranking individuals. What could she possibly have said that would rise to the level of a Code Orange?

"There are rules for reviews on those sites, so I take it her reviews did not contain profanity."

"No, but they weren't what a member of the royal family would post." Zeno unfolded a printout, apparently a screen shot of a review. "This is for a toaster oven."

As Zeno held the paper aloft and prepared to read, Sergio turned around and coughed. Then Margaret started laughing and mumbled a, "Pardon me, Your Highness."

Zeno turned in the seat so he couldn't see Margaret or Sergio as he read aloud. "This toaster oven does, indeed, toast a variety of items. Unfortunately, one cannot eat anything after this toaster oven has been used—even other food—because the stench created when you hit the power button is overwhelming. I don't know if faulty wiring or faulty components are to blame, but if you value your mealtime, do not click the buy button. You may as well take your meal into the midst of a fetid garbage dump to eat, because the odor from this toaster oven will permeate your taste buds, if not your entire kitchen. You'll feel like you're surrounded by rotting fish and other waste as you eat. PS: On a positive note, if you happen to receive this toaster oven as a housewarming gift, you'll quickly meet your new neighbors and perhaps your local firefighters when they come to investigate the noxious fumes."

Sergio's face went crimson as he fought to contain his laughter.

Zeno lowered the paper. "The toaster oven manufacturer has been the subject of online, well, I'll call it mockery, Your Highness. There were other reviews in a similar vein. A shorter one was for a ten-year battery. She noted that it lasted three weeks in her smoke detector, but made a nice ten-year ornament on her Christmas tree after she removed it from the detector, tested it to confirm that it was dead, and then tied a ribbon to the top."

Eduardo bit back a grin and tapped his fingers against the desktop. "So humorous, but nothing salacious. And no false claims about any of the items."

"Correct, Your Highness. A true Code Orange. If the reviews hadn't contained humor, I doubt they'd have caught anyone's attention. But now that they have, they're being repeated. I'll be asked about them in the press room today."

Eduardo leaned back in his chair. "This solves one of the great mysteries of the universe. We now know how Amanda and Marco found common ground to marry."

"Please say I can use that," Zeno begged. "Not quoting you, of course, Your Highness. I'd prefer to steal it."

"If you think it will help defuse the situation, be my guest. Now are we finished?"

When everyone said they were set, Eduardo stood. He could see in their expressions that, while the Code Orange issue had drawn some of the tension from the room, his senior staff remained concerned about his relationship with Claire and what it could mean for the Strada il Teatro project.

"All right. Priority number one this week is the Strada. Zeno, please drive that home to the media. Margaret, when you meet with any groups who have an interest in the appearance of the Strada—say, one of the museum foundations or theater charities—let them know how excited we are about the proposed plan and remind them that we're all in this together. We don't want them to see us as an adversary, but as a partner in protecting their interests for the future. We want their support to remain strong."

"I will, Your Highness."

"And Sergio, you know what to do. Finalize whatever sections of the plan you can so we can provide supportive members of parliament with an early preview. When the formal plan is introduced and it's time for us to take a step back, I want them primed to argue in favor of it."

At Sergio's nod of understanding, Eduardo planted his hands on the desk. "This is important. You all know why. It's also important to me personally."

He looked at them one by one, needing to drive the point home. "I married a wonderful woman in Queen Aletta. Each of you know what she meant to me and what she meant to this country. It's right that people wish to honor her legacy. That being said, I don't want my sole legacy to be that I had a beloved wife. I want future generations to know that I used the valuable time I was given in this office to improve San Rimini. I want to inspire them to do the same. Now let's get this done."

CHAPTER 18

"I CAN'T BELIEVE it took us this long." Claire said as she pointed Eduardo toward the cabinet that contained her glassware. She salted the popcorn and held the large bowl in front of her to give the contents a gentle air toss. She'd insisted that they do this movie theater style. She'd even managed to locate two boxes of Raisinets at a specialty shop on her way home from work.

Eduardo's mouth had twisted in disdain when she'd presented the candy upon his arrival. He'd noted that any number of confectionaries in town could have made chocolate-covered raisins to order and she needn't have purchased the packaged variety.

"You've never had Raisinets, have you?" she'd asked.

"No."

"Then it's about time."

"You sound like Samuel Barden trying to convince me to try a new sweet potato recipe."

"We've waited this long to watch the movie. Do you think I'd ruin it with candy I know you won't like?"

"Hmm. This will be a test of my trust in you."

She'd given him a playful kiss and urged him into the kitchen.

Over a late-night dinner at a Greek restaurant the previous week, she'd teased him about his inability to get *Out of Africa* at the palace. In the end, it was Luisa who discovered that the film was between licenses in San Rimini. The previous broadcaster had dropped it, but another had it scheduled to begin in two months.

Claire had searched online until she found a way to do a one-time rental. They'd blocked off the evening in each of their calendars and agreed to watch the movie at her place. Now the opening scene was ready to go, paused on the television as they assembled their snacks.

They were going to do this the right way.

Eduardo capped the soda, then returned the bottle to the fridge. As she located the napkins, she told him, "I saw the transportation minister on the news earlier. He was talking about your plan for the Strada il Teatro."

"Sergio tells me he is enthusiastic. I hope that was apparent?"

"He told the reporter that he'd recently met with members of the Central Business District Council to discuss the current version and that all involved felt that it was a carefully considered plan—that was his phrase. If parliament were to pass it, he said that the country could look forward to an improved downtown area without sacrificing the aspects that make it a national treasure."

"That's music to my ears." He accepted a few napkins from Claire, then started toward the sitting room with the napkins and soda. She followed with the popcorn. The Raisinets were already on the coffee table. As he placed the drinks on coasters, he said, "The plan goes to parliament next week. Officially, that is. The key players have seen the latest draft so they're ready to speak to its components once it's out of our hands and the budget discussion begins."

She reached for the switch on a tall lamp that stood beside the sofa and doused the light before picking up the remote. "Do you think it will pass as is?"

"My staff did the dirty work of herding the cats so they're all facing the same direction. Parliament knows it's needed and that they'll never have an opportunity with less political risk. But they need to move on it before anyone decides to change direction. If that happens, they're in for a slog. No one wants that."

Eduardo settled into the cushions, then put one arm along the back of the sofa, inviting her to settle against him. She took a seat and was about to start the movie when Eduardo noticed a box in the corner. "You have an entire carton of champagne. Is that for me?"

"Not in the way you think." She'd planned to tell him later in the week, but she supposed it didn't matter. "Mark Rosenburg has a follow-up meeting with Sonia Selvaggi on Monday. She has a few remaining questions about teacher security. Mark's going to walk her through the protocols that are already in place, plus some that will be added as the program expands into areas where the concerns are different."

He leaned back so he could see her face. "You're going to get her support?"

"We are. I've spoken with her twice, once on the phone and once in person. Mark's done the heavy lifting. She's all but told him she's a yes vote should you introduce it to parliament. As soon as Mark has her agreement, I'm taking that case of champagne to his office so he can it share with his team, except for the last bottle, which we will send to you."

"You have an evil streak, you know that?"

She winked and lifted the remote. As the opening credits began, she cuddled against him. "Speaking of evil, how did your cribbage game go with Giovanni last weekend?"

"That evil streak of yours is getting wider and wider."

"I like to play dirty sometimes."

"Now that sounds fun."

She clicked the remote and the screen went to a wide shot of a hazy orange sunset and a single tree. Gradually, the silhouette of a hunter appeared against the low, desolate sun. Claire knew the first lines by heart, about Karen Blixen's memory of a man who took his gramophone on safari.

Three rifles, supplies for a month, and Mozart.

Claire wrapped her arms around Eduardo's waist and allowed herself to be carried away by the music, the story, and Eduardo's strong embrace.

LATER, long after they'd abandoned popcorn and Raisinets in favor of a warm bed, Claire lay on her back with her eyes closed and Eduardo's cheek against her breast. His chest rose and fell with hers and the day's growth of facial hair rasped against her skin. His heart thudded against hers in a reassuring rhythm and a light sheen of sweat evaporated from his back into the cool air. Her fingers dragged back and forth across his hair as she cherished all of it.

Exhausted as they were, she knew he was awake and savoring it, too.

When she slowed the movement, he turned his head and planted a delicate kiss at the base of her throat.

"Do you need to go home?" she whispered.

"No. Are you kicking me out?"

She skimmed her fingertips along the back of his neck and between his shoulder blades, which drew a satisfied murmur. "Never. This feels too good to let go."

He nipped at her throat before pushing to his elbows and bracing them on either side of her. "Not that I don't appreciate all that came before it, but this moment is special. With you. Thank you."

She smiled at that as she continued to caress his back. "Later this week, when I'm in my office with a long list of phone calls to make and people and projects demanding my attention, this is what I'll come to in my mind for peace."

He closed his eyes and inhaled slowly, as if drawing fortification for his own week, then lowered himself until his forehead rested against hers. There was an enormity to the moment; they lay like that for several seconds, then he brushed his lips over hers in a kiss that felt as if it held years of checked emotion.

Afterward, he remained still. When she opened her eyes, he held her gaze as if he'd been waiting for her. "Sex I've never had a problem with, at least not in theory. Intimacy, however, is something else. It's rare for anyone. Rarer still for anyone with jobs like ours. The risks are too great."

He shifted slightly, but didn't take his eyes off hers. "I've fallen in love with you, Claire Peyton. The thought of you excites me, but it also brings me peace. I so deeply believed that I'd never experience that feeling after Aletta died that I didn't bother to look for it. But when we met, I recognized that I could have it with you. Perhaps even the night we danced at the credentials ceremony. You captivated me."

"What, when you thought I'd been about to commit a faux pas and ask you to dance?"

He brushed a stray tendril of hair from her forehead and smiled. "I could have evaded. I didn't. I wanted to dance with you. In fact, I wanted it very badly."

Claire felt tears pooling in her eyes. She didn't want to blink, knowing they'd spill over, but Eduardo saw them coming and used his thumbs to blot them away.

"I love you, Eduardo. I trust you. And I'm very glad I had the opportunity to dance with you."

He kissed her again, then said, "You were worth the wait."

It made her enormously happy to hear, but at the same time, her heart broke for him and all he'd been through.

"You mentioned that you haven't dated since Aletta passed away. But surely in that time...you haven't...?"

All the diplomatic skills in the world didn't help her phrase the question she wanted to ask, but Eduardo understood.

"It's been nine years for that, too. Well, more." He eased to the side, drawing her with him so they faced each other in the dark.

On a long breath, he said, "Off and on for several months, Aletta mentioned having intestinal issues and feeling bloated. Depending on the day, she attributed it to a busy schedule, to a meal that disagreed with her, or to the pressures of preparing for Federico's wedding. It was nothing that interfered with her daily life, merely an annoyance. A routine exam raised a flag. That turned into multiple follow-ups, during which we learned she had advanced ovarian cancer. Federico's wedding fell in the midst of the follow-up appointments. While the country was wrapped up in photos of the wedding gown and who

Federico would ask to be his best man, Aletta and I entered crisis mode."

He traced a path along Claire's side until he found a comfortable spot on her hip to settle his hand. "Life became a cascade of decisions. How and when to tell our children. How to tell her sister, Helena, who was also her personal assistant. We had to manage doctors' visits and surgery and chemotherapy, and figure out what the staff and then the public needed to know and when, all while trying to put Aletta's mental and physical health first. It was stressful and agonizing, and I certainly wasn't thinking about...well, anything else. And I was scared for her."

As Claire listened to Eduardo, her respect and love for him grew. Aletta's treatment was the most advanced available at the time. They'd tried to be optimistic, to tell themselves that there were brighter days ahead. By the time they knew Aletta wouldn't be cured, sex was the last thing on their minds. She was in no condition physically and neither of them were in that place emotionally. From the day of Aletta's diagnosis until the day Claire had walked into Eduardo's palace apartment to tell him she thought they should end their relationship —and they'd ended up in bed instead—he'd been celibate.

And, Claire was certain, he'd kept his pain to himself. He couldn't hide the fact he was in mourning. But after the initial shock of his wife's death, in the long years he'd spent alone and dedicated to his job, he spoke of it to no one. Not his children. Not his siblings. Not even Giovanni.

Claire placed a hand on his chest. Her fingers brushed the edge of his scar. "That's a long time."

One side of his mouth lifted in agreement. "I was married to the most wonderful woman I'd ever met. The whole world knew it. There was no bringing that back. But at the same time, the experience drove home the lesson that life is fragile. My father died of a congenital defect and I'd been tested years before, so I knew I had the same issue and would likely need surgery at some point. A few years after Aletta's death, my cardiovascular capacity suddenly dropped like a stone. I had the perpetual feeling that I was going to die, even though I could see on the scans that I wasn't. My cardiovascular surgeon assured me that even though the surgery carried risks, I was an ideal candidate. I'd stayed in shape, never smoked, and ate a fairly healthy diet." He rolled his eyes, then added, "Not as healthy as what Samuel insists on now, but overall, I was in good shape. In any case, my doctors warned me that decreased cardio capacity can trigger feelings of doom, but the sensation was petrifying. When I woke up following the surgery and the medication wore off, I was in the worst pain of my life, but that feeling of doom was gone. Recovery became my mission. I wanted to live. I wanted to accomplish things. I wanted to enjoy my children and grandchildren and experience all the richness of life while I could."

"But you didn't date."

His fingers flexed against her hip. "I didn't think I'd find the intimacy I had with Aletta. Even if I could, I knew it wouldn't be easy to find a woman who'd be comfortable dating me and all it entails. There's no getting around the sheer opulence and tradition of the palace. Some people crave that type of environment, but others find it uncomfortable. There's a lack of privacy, too. You know what it's like. When anyone enters or leaves, dozens of people know. And it's not only my security team or my staff; my children also live under that roof. When I have a guest, they're aware of it. And then there's the media."

She acknowledged that with a tilt of the head. "And then there's the media. It's not only a matter of privacy where they're concerned. They handed you a certain reputation. That must have played into it."

"Ah, yes, the man known as a romantic icon? The venerable widower?"

"I would never phrase it that way."

"The rest of the world does. Even so, my reputation shouldn't play into my decisions."

"But it does." He knew as well as she did that in politics, reputation affected one's ability to accomplish goals. It couldn't be completely ignored, even in one's private life.

"It does," he admitted. "If I'd wanted to date casually, I probably could have found a way to do so with minimal risk. Miroslav or Chiara could have managed it. But that's just not me. And when I met the right woman, I didn't want it to be casual."

"Were you lonely?"

He was quiet for several seconds. "I live a busy life and I enjoy what I do. I have a purpose. I have friends. But yes. I was lonely. I did a fine job of not thinking about it for a long time. But I didn't ask you for the opera date because I was lonely."

He covered her hand where she'd flattened it against her chest. "I was debating the risks of asking you out when I learned that Amanda and Marco are expecting a child. It isn't public knowledge, but Amanda carries multiple mutated genes that make her prone to breast and ovarian cancer. She and Marco had long discussions with doctors about preventive measures and about the pros and cons of having children. They decided to try for one child and to give it six to nine months, then stop. She became pregnant after seven months. I didn't know the details of her medical history until they told me about the pregnancy. But they wanted me to understand why they waited until the last possible moment to make the public announcement."

He smiled and kissed her fingertips. "Marco said that we only live life once, and that he and Amanda hoped to live it with a child. They were willing to take a calculated risk. When he said that, I knew I felt the same about you. That night, I told Giovanni I wanted to ask you for a date. I knew before I talked to him that I would, but it felt better to have his encouragement."

"I always knew I liked him." She scooted closer, then added, "But I like you more. Stay for pancakes?"

He glanced at the clock on her nightstand, then grinned. "Pancakes? At midnight?"

"I was thinking around seven or eight. Nine, if you care to sleep late."

His hand moved from her hip to her rear and he pulled her flush to his body. "Let me give security a quick call. Then I'm all yours."

CHAPTER 19

HALF AN HOUR after Eduardo talked to his security team, his cell phone rang.

Claire heard it first and stretched to retrieve it from the nightstand.

"They said a ten a.m. pickup wouldn't be a problem," he murmured, his brain foggy from the first moments of sleep.

"Missed something on your schedule, maybe?"

He grunted a no. Other than an evening phone call to congratulate members of the University of San Rimini's robotics team, which had finished third in a worldwide competition, his day was clear. He'd planned to spend it reading his briefing book and catching up on correspondence.

He accepted the phone from Claire, then put it to his ear. *"Pronto?"*

"Your Highness, I realize it's after midnight, but your security chief told me she believed you were still awake."

Eduardo recognized the voice as that of his defense ministry liaison. He sat up, suddenly alert. "What has happened?"

"You remember the accident that took place on the Strada il Teatro about three months ago? We've had another a block west. A family of five walked from their hotel to the park near the stairs that connect the Strada to the Via Vespri to see fireworks from a wedding taking place near the marina. On their return, they entered the crosswalk at the top of the stairs and were struck. The driver was looking at the opposite side of the street and failed to see them. He stopped and provided assistance, but their injuries are grave. A group of men exiting one of the casinos began yelling at the driver and dragged him to the sidewalk. He had already called emergency services and the police arrived before the altercation went too far. The driver hit his head on the curb and may have broken ribs, but the initial report is that he will be all right. His attackers have been detained. There are two ambulances on the scene assisting the family. The media are on the way and will be held a few blocks from the accident. However, given that the accident will shut down the Strada for at least an hour as the situation is sorted, you needed to be informed."

"Do you know the condition of the family?"

"Not yet, Your Highness. As of now, there are no reported fatalities, but the situation is fluid."

"Keep me updated."

Eduardo dropped the phone and rubbed a hand over his face. This was his nightmare.

"I heard," Claire said. "Do you want to go back to the palace to wait for news?"

"I just sent my driver home."

"Mine lives a few blocks away. He told me he rarely goes to bed before two or three. Let me send him a quick message. He's worked for the embassy for years and understands security protocols."

Eduardo hesitated, but only for a second. "If he's available, that's fine. Otherwise, I'll call mine back."

He found his clothing and headed for the bathroom. When he emerged, the lamp was on and Claire was sitting on the edge of the bed, fully dressed. "Fabiano is on his way."

Eduardo reached for her hand. "A family of five means children."

She kissed his knuckles. "I'll come with you."

He nodded, then they went to the front door to wait.

Fabiano took them to La Rocca using side streets, but every so often Eduardo caught glimpses of the emergency lights on the Strada il Teatro.

Claire followed his gaze, then reached for his knee and gave him a reassuring squeeze before flipping her palm to hold his hand.

When security waved the car through the rear entrance, he told her, "I need to go to my office. I could be a while."

"I'll send Fabiano home and find a spot to wait." She held her phone aloft. "I have a few documents I can read."

Sergio and Zeno were talking outside his office when he arrived. He should have been surprised to see them, but somehow he wasn't. "You heard?"

Sergio nodded. "My wife and I had dinner near the marina, then stayed to watch fireworks from a wedding. We heard the sirens and I called to see what was happening. Zeno received a media alert and decided to come in."

Sergio offered to make coffee and the men settled around the coffee table in Eduardo's office to wait for news.

They sat in silence for several minutes, then Sergio said, "You were at Claire Peyton's home, Your Highness?"

Zeno's head snapped up, as if he couldn't believe Sergio had asked the question when they both knew the answer.

"I was."

Sergio ran his index finger around the rim of his coffee cup. "She has Selvaggi, doesn't she? I heard a rumor."

"She does. Not officially, but it's coming."

This time, the silence fell like a weight.

"No matter what we hear from the hospital tonight, this is a tragedy." Sergio was hesitant, picking his words with care. "A family will be devastated by this, even if they all survive. The driver will be forever changed. Tourists will worry about their safety."

"We can't fix tonight, much as we might wish it. We can only move forward."

"Yes, Your Highness." Sergio swallowed, then said, "Tonight's tragedy points out why the improvements are necessary. But if Ambassador Peyton gets Sonia Selvaggi's support and you introduce that legislation, it will not go over well, particularly at a time when you need the public to believe in you and your vision."

Eduardo shook his head. "We won't sabotage her talks with Selvaggi, if that's what you're suggesting. The timing isn't ideal, I'll grant you, but what she's arguing for is legislation I support. You support it, Sergio. It's the *traditional* role of the monarch to promote these kinds of programs."

"Yes, Your Highness. But given the circumstances, you need to postpone it. We've had to devote so much time and effort in the Strada project precisely because it's *not* the type of legislation in which San Rimini's monarchs involve themselves. The commitments we have are fragile. If it's going to go through, you need the public's support. If San Rimini's citizens believe you're making a choice for your girlfriend's sake, no matter how viable that choice, your popularity will plummet even more than it already has and you'll be in a Catch-22. You won't be able to fix the very thing they need fixed."

"Sergio, I gave my word."

Sergio said nothing, but his jaw clenched.

Zeno said, "You did give your word, Your Highness. But not only to Ambassador Peyton."

Eduardo closed his eyes. He'd promised he'd have Claire's back. He'd said it the very night she'd received a call from the President checking to be sure she had her priorities straight.

His phone vibrated in his pocket. Almost simultaneously, Zeno received an alert and said he needed to make a call. As Eduardo answered, Sergio's phone rang. They separated, each moving to a different section of the room so they could hear.

The news was grim. The driver had a concussion, a cracked rib. and a possible eye injury and would be admitted for observation. The family consisted of a mother, father, two children, and the mother's sister. The mother and her sister had minor injuries and were being treated and released. One of the children, a girl, was receiving stitches to cuts on her back and one leg. She would likely be released by morning. The father had been carrying the second child, also a girl. They'd suffered the most worrisome injuries. Both had hit their heads on the pavement. The girl's head injury didn't appear to be severe, but her arm and collarbone had been broken and the arm required surgery. The father had a broken pelvis and several broken ribs. He was still being examined to determine the extent of his head injury.

Police remained on the Strada il Teatro as part of the accident investigation, but would clear the scene and reopen the street by sunrise.

He ended the call shortly after Sergio and Zeno finished theirs. They compared notes; all had received the same information, albeit from different sources.

Zeno asked Eduardo if he wanted to make a statement in the morning, given the high profile of the Strada il Teatro. He nodded, then said, "I doubt we'll hear anything for another hour or two. You should sleep while you can. I'm going to take a walk through the garden and clear my head, then I'll draft a statement for your input."

With that, Eduardo turned and made his way outside.

The air was cool, forcing him to shake his arms so his sleeves covered his wrists before he shoved his hands into his front pockets. His right thumb hit velvet and tears stung his eyes. He shook off the sensation and strode along the gravel path toward the fountain. He wasn't surprised to see Claire sitting on a bench facing the pool.

She lowered her phone as he approached. When he sat beside her, she said nothing. He stared at the water for several seconds. He ached for Claire, but couldn't bring himself to touch her. As if on cue, she turned sideways and kicked her legs across his lap, then wrapped her arms around his shoulders and kissed his temple.

"Three adults, two children," he said. "The father has unknown head injuries, a broken pelvis and broken ribs. A little girl is in surgery for a broken arm. The others are injured, but will be all right. The driver will likely be all right, but he has a concussion and a possible eye injury."

She cupped his cheek and pressed another kiss to his temple. "You're a good man, Eduardo diTalora."

"It doesn't feel that way."

"You care. You're doing all you can to prevent an accident from happening again. That's more than most people can say."

"Am I doing all I can? I don't know. And I don't know if I have the strength."

He'd made a promise to Claire, but he owed his allegiance to his country first. It was what Sergio and Zeno had wanted to say, but hadn't.

The citizens of San Rimini relied on him to make wise choices. Where safety on the Strada il Teatro was concerned, that meant hundreds of thousands of people, perhaps millions, given that the changes would affect the area for decades to come. What was that when weighed against educational legislation that he could postpone for later, once the Strada changes had passed through parliament?

But if he reneged on the deal he'd made with Claire, he could very well lose her. It wasn't a straightforward matter of her being mad at him or feeling lied to. His decision could ruin her professionally. The President had appointed her to a coveted job because of the work she'd done on education in Uganda, and with the understanding that she would continue that work. It was the cornerstone of his campaign when he'd run for office.

More than that, the issue spoke to Claire personally. Her mother and two uncles had worked their way out of poverty because they'd been presented educational opportunities and scholarships through similar programs. Claire had mentioned more than once that she owed her career to her parents and the example they'd set. It was who she was. It was one of the many traits that made him love her.

He enveloped her in a hug.

Lightning had struck him twice in his life. First with Aletta, and now with Claire. He couldn't hold on to it the first time. If he didn't hold on now, he'd never be the same again.

He closed his eyes and took a long, deep breath. He needed to imprint the feel of her on his mind.

Then he let go.

His throat tightened as if he were being choked by the weight of the world. "Claire, I—"

"You know what you have to do, Eduardo."

Her eyes searched his, then she said it again.

He couldn't believe what he was hearing. "Claire, I made a promise. So did you, to the President of the United States."

"Yes, I did. I promised to address a number of issues during my tenure here, involving everything from defense to business to the environment to education. I also promised him that I'd avoid a conflict of interest. I have no intention of going back on my word."

"I need to postpone our deal, Claire. If you agree to that, I don't see how that's avoiding a conflict of interest."

He didn't miss the tremor of her lower lip, but when she spoke, it was with the same clarity that had earned her the respect of both her coworkers and his family.

"You bought me an olive tree. It's a symbol of peace. But you and I both know that peace isn't easy. Peace means that, at times, you have to be a good partner. In this case, the United States needs to be a good partner to San Rimini. That means allowing the king to prioritize another issue so that we can count on his full, unwavering support for the education program when he introduces it to parliament at a later date, when his popularity is high because he's ushered in a project his country has needed for a long, long time. By giving the king this latitude, I'm confident that we will have his support on future projects, as well."

Emotion rippled through his voice despite his effort to control it. "You sound like a rather accomplished diplomat. I could take some lessons from you."

Her eyes brightened with tears and she smiled. "I do my best."

"It may not be enough. You could still lose your job. Your job is your purpose, Claire."

"I've thought about that a lot lately. I've come to the conclusion that, job or no job, I have a purpose. I might not have the same platform, but I have the desire and the drive. I don't have to be an ambassador to continue helping others. It's no different than what your family does on a daily basis. Or any of the thousands of people who work for causes that matter to them." Her mouth lifted into a smile.

"Do you remember at the opera, when you told me you were old enough to know your heart and your mind? I know mine, too. This is the right thing."

"Claire, I don't know what to say."

"Say that you love me."

He buried his hands in her hair and kissed her. There was heat to it, but one that was borne of trust and love. A love that was growing deeper and deeper every day. Between kisses, he said the words over and over.

When he finally paused long enough to press his forehead to hers, she said, "You should go back inside. If there's more news, your staff will come looking for you."

"Soon," he said, then kissed her again. "I want to do something else first."

"You can kiss me later. If you play your cards right, you can do a lot more."

"No. Not that. I want you to marry me."

She blinked and pulled back. "What?"

He'd surprised himself with the words, but he meant every one of them. He couldn't help but smile at the astonishment on her face.

"I want you to marry me, Claire, but on your timeline. You can't be married to me and hold your job. So do the work you love for as long as you wish to, or until you can't. When you're ready for a change, I'll be here. You can pursue any philanthropic interest you want as a member of my family." He took a deep breath, then added, "On the other hand, it isn't easy being a member of a royal family. It comes with the expectations of an entire country. If you don't wish to take on that burden by marrying me, I understand. But I hope you'll stay in San Rimini and I hope you'll stay with me. I don't want to live another day of my life without you in it."

"Oh, Eduardo. I don't want to live without you, either. It would break my heart."

He eased from the bench, then knelt before her, holding her hands between his as she looked at him in amazement. "Claire Peyton, would you do me the deep honor of being my wife?"

They heard the crunch of gravel at the same time. They looked toward the palace, then back at each other. When their eyes caught, they smothered their laughter. "You have to be kidding me," Claire whispered. "Quick, get up before they see you."

He angled his head, waiting.

"Yes! The answer is yes! Now get up or it'll be palace gossip within the hour. We need time for this to be between the two of us."

When Sergio came into view, Eduardo had resumed his seat beside Claire. Given the weightlessness he felt on the inside, he was proud of how sedate he looked on the outside.

"You have news?"

"The father's head injury isn't as bad as originally feared. He's undergoing surgery to repair his pelvis now and the doctors are optimistic. Apparently, it's as good a break as one can have in the situation. The daughter is out of surgery. No complications thus far. They'll both need time to heal, but no one is critical."

"That's very good to hear. As soon as they're able to have visitors, I'll have Luisa make arrangements. Quietly, though. Given the tenuousness of the Strada project, I don't want it to come off as a public relations stunt."

"I think that would be welcome, Your Highness." Sergio smiled at Claire, and said, "It's good to see you, Madam Ambassador."

"And you as well, Sergio, though not under these circumstances. If I haven't said it before, thank you for all you do for King Eduardo. I'm reassured knowing that you're watching out for him."

Sergio blinked, then tipped his head as if to say, *and the same to you.*

He stood still for a moment, then turned to Eduardo. "I'll check in tomorrow with any updates. Otherwise, assuming you survive Greta, I'll see you for our Monday morning meeting."

"I'll do my best," Eduardo promised.

When Sergio was out of sight, Eduardo turned to Claire. "I think you just planted another olive tree. Now, where were we?"

She lifted her hand to his face and traced a path along his cheekbone, first with her index finger, then with her thumb, before cradling his cheek. "I believe you were about to ask me to dance."

"Without music?"

"We can imagine."

"Imagine it with this, then." He reached into his pocket and withdrew the small velvet bag he'd tucked there that evening, and on several other evenings over the past two weeks. He knew he'd offer it to Claire, but he wasn't sure when. He took her hand, then opened the bag and overturned it so the ring fell into her open palm.

"It belonged to my great-grandmother," he said. "When you're ready for this to be public, I hope you'll wear it."

She looked at him with tears in her eyes, then at the ring. She ran a finger over the emerald and the small diamonds that surrounded it. "Eduardo, this is exquisite." She slid it onto her finger, and they were both surprised to see that it fit.

"Do you mind if I wear it tonight?"

"I would love that."

He stood, extended a hand, then whirled her into his arms. Their feet moved together, and as her fingertips brushed his nape, he knew they heard the same song in their minds.

It was everything he could ever want. The stars sparkling overhead. The woman he loved in his arms. His children and grandchildren asleep in the palace that surrounded the garden.

He tightened his hold and pressed a kiss to Claire's temple.

He was at peace.

EPILOGUE

EDUARDO LEANED FORWARD and waved as he rode along the Strada il Teatro in an open-top carriage. Beside him, Claire perched on the red velvet seat, her eyes glowing with excitement. One hand rested atop the polished black door while the other held his. She wore an ivory silk gown, a tiara that had belonged to his mother, and a pair of turquoise and silver earrings that had been crafted by a childhood friend of her own mother's. A matching turquoise and silver bracelet circled her wrist.

Her emerald and diamond engagement ring sparkled on her left hand.

All around them, crowds whistled and cheered under a bright, sunny sky.

Every so often, Claire pressed a hand to her heart, then waved. Happiness rolled off her.

A decade earlier, he'd walked this same route behind the 1750 State Coach, a gilt-laden vehicle so massive that it required a team of six horses to navigate San Rimini's cobblestoned streets.

It had been empty as it wound its way to the Duomo that day, a traditional final farewell to a member of the royal family. The three hours that followed that walk had been the longest of Eduardo's life as he'd endured the memorial service at the Duomo and then a reception at the palace. He'd felt as if his soul had been ripped from his body, leaving a void that could never be filled.

He would always mourn Aletta. But as with the Strada il Teatro, which would soon be torn apart and rebuilt for a new era, so too had his soul undergone a renewal.

He had the woman beside him to thank for it. She had taught him to live in the present, and every moment of the past two months had driven that home. Next month, he planned to thank her by introducing legislation that would send funds and teachers to the education program she'd championed in Uganda.

Two months ago, Claire had stepped down from her office. Though she'd been certain the President would want a political ally to fill the role, he'd followed her recommendation and promoted from within the embassy, elevating Mark Rosenburg to the position. Claire couldn't have been more thrilled. Karen Hutchinson had offered to stay on and work with Mark's assistant during the transition, but planned to leave afterward.

Though Karen had kept it quiet at work, Claire had confided that Karen was involved with King Eduardo's defense ministry liaison, a man she'd apparently described to Claire as "good looking" at the credentials ceremony. They'd bonded over their government jobs, thirst for travel, and love of baking. They both wanted children and Claire suspected a wedding would be in the works soon.

Two weeks after Claire left office, Zeno Amendola had strolled into his usual Monday morning press briefing and given updates about the Strada il Teatro project before announcing plans for Prince Antony to visit Belgium as part of San Rimini's delegation at an upcoming climate summit. When Zeno opened the floor for questions, he'd fully expected the barrage that hit him to address everything but those two items.

Claire had appeared on a roundtable American political program the day before to discuss the worldwide refugee crisis. However, the moderator had quickly pivoted to personal matters when speaking to Claire.

"You recently retired from your role as the United States Ambassador to San Rimini. There's now talk that you and King Eduardo could marry. San Riminians have strong opinions about that."

"Do they?" Claire's laugh was genuine, her eyes sparkling as she faced the moderator.

"Particularly in regard to a title."

"Well, I've lived a good portion of my life with a title. It has been an honor to be called Madam Ambassador. I have no need or desire for another."

"Are you saying you've discussed this with the king? Do you have plans to marry?"

"I'm saying exactly what I just stated. It was an honor to serve as the American ambassador to San Rimini. I was able to forge partnerships that benefit both our countries. I had the opportunity to meet and work with some incredible people, many of whom have become dear friends. And while I've retired from my role as ambassador, I have no intention to stop working. I plan to pursue a number of philanthropic projects that are near and dear to my heart. I haven't seen a study on the subject, but I suspect many career diplomats do the same. A desire to make a difference is what brought many of us to the state department in the first place." She'd turned to another panelist and said, "Wouldn't you agree, Ronald? What drew you to your career and to the issue of refugees in particular?"

The interview clip had aired on nearly every network in Europe. Overnight, the public perception of Claire changed. Even the most barbed tabloid reporters commented on her political acumen and her history of helping those in need, rather than labeling her as a fortune hunter merely angling for the late queen's title.

As the questions hit from multiple reporters, Zeno held his hands palms out in a request for silence in the briefing room. When it quieted, he broke into a huge smile. "I have news to share that I believe will answer your questions. It is my pleasure to announce that

King Eduardo and the Honorable Claire Peyton are engaged to be married. They plan to wed at a private ceremony here at the palace in approximately six weeks. Other details will be forthcoming, but in the meantime, let's close this briefing by wishing them a long and happy life together."

The room had erupted.

As Zeno had announced, their wedding had taken place in the palace chapel. Karen Hutchinson had served as maid of honor and Giovanni Sozzani had served as best man. The guests had included Claire's family, who'd flown in from New Mexico, staff members from La Rocca and the embassy, and a number of friends. The entire diTalora clan was in attendance, though Eduardo heard so many people ask both Arturo and Paolo whether they had gum he feared they might mount an escape. King Carlo and Queen Fabrizia had come from Sarcaccia, as had Queen Fabrizia's personal assistant, Daniela, and her husband, Royce, who'd both done work for Eduardo several years earlier. After he'd introduced Daniela and Royce to Claire, Eduardo had leaned close and whispered, "I have to tell you their story. Don't let me forget."

It had been a personal, uplifting ceremony, and as he and Claire exited the chapel and walked toward the carriage that would take them through the streets of San Rimini for a celebratory ride, he'd felt as if he were walking on air.

Yes, Eduardo thought, the choices they'd made leading up to the ceremony were perfect for the two of them.

The previous morning, Miroslav had spirited them out of the palace so they could visit the Duomo together before it opened at sunrise. They'd left flowers for Aletta—a happy, colorful bouquet rather than the usual white roses—and hadn't been surprised to see that a number of others had left flowers in recent days. As Eduardo had turned to go, Claire had asked to remain alone for a moment. He'd watched her speak softly in front of the crypt, her hands folded in front of her, while he'd waited in a nearby pew. Then he'd allowed his gaze to lift to the stained-glass windows. They remained dark in the predawn hours, but he knew the stories they told. They were tales of hope, of family, of kindness. Of love.

It was as he'd promised Aletta when he'd visited on the last anniversary of her passing. This visit was more meaningful and there were no cameras. This was as it should be.

Claire had approached soundlessly and put a hand on his shoulder. "Onward?"

"Onward."

Last night they'd enjoyed dinner in the residence with Claire's parents, his four children and their spouses, and King Carlo and Queen Fabrizia. Though Eduardo didn't need Queen Fabrizia's blessing before marrying Claire, it had meant the world to him when, at the end of the night, his wife's dearest friend had confided, "Aletta would have loved her. I can see that your children do. I'm so happy for you, Eduardo. Carlo and I both are. She's wonderful."

Afterward, when they were alone, he'd held Claire for a long time. They were both too keyed up to sleep, so they'd found a comedy show on television and curled up on the sofa. They'd talked about the wedding, about the guests, and about Claire's new role. She had a purpose, but one that wouldn't be dictated by a president or state department. She'd gotten to know Margaret Halaby, and together they'd discussed philanthropic pursuits that appealed to Claire. Her first project involved promoting a clinic in Ethiopia that offered treatment to women who'd suffered from fistulas during childbirth. Both Amanda and Jennifer, Prince Antony's wife, hoped to become involved in the project, which had thrilled Claire. In the coming months, Claire hoped to visit the clinic in person, then travel on to Uganda to visit one of the schools she'd toured early in her time as ambassador to that country.

The carriage turned onto another street, making a wide loop around the block containing the American embassy. As the building came into sight, Claire squeezed his hand.

It was an acknowledgment that, though they'd each faced challenges and heartbreak to get to this point, their trust in each other and their love would carry them forward.

When the carriage turned back onto the Strada il Teatro for another pass through the crowd and a return to La Rocca, Eduardo leaned over and kissed his bride. She smiled and kissed him right back.

He'd come full circle.

All in all, it was a beautiful life.

ACKNOWLEDGMENTS

My sincere thanks to everyone who has embraced the Royal Scandals: San Rimini series and the diTalora royal family. My wonderful editors, Holly Ingraham and Gail Chasan, and my proofreader, Robin Phillips of Author Help UK, have provided valuable insights on the series and teach me something new with each title. I'm fortunate to have Hollis McCarthy, a talented performer and storyteller, bring the audio editions of my books to life. The cover art for the entire series was designed by the fantastic Patricia Schmitt, and I can't say enough positive things about my website and newsletter team at Xuni.com – Madeira James, Riley Mack, and Ryan Chrys.

I also owe a deep debt of gratitude to my readers. Thank you to all of you who've read the stories, shared with friends, posted reviews, and sent me email. Without you, none of the rest would be possible.

Finally, thank you to my writer friends and to my family for all you do. Emily March, Linda Winstead Jones, and Christina Dodd have served as brainstorming partners and cheerleaders for many years. My husband and kids have run to answer numerous panicked cries of, "someone get the dog!" and "one of you answer the phone!" when I'm knee deep in a scene and need to concentrate in order to pull a story out of the mud. They've handled more make-your-own-dinner nights than I care to admit and, thankfully, they do their own laundry. It's their support that allows me the freedom to build worlds and find adventure there.

ALSO BY NICOLE BURNHAM

ROYAL SCANDALS

Christmas With a Prince (prequel novella)

Scandal With a Prince

Honeymoon With a Prince

Christmas on the Royal Yacht (novella)

Slow Tango With a Prince

The Royal Bastard

Christmas With a Palace Thief (novella)

The Wicked Prince

One Man's Princess

ROYAL SCANDALS: SAN RIMINI

Fit for a Queen

Going to the Castle

The Prince's Tutor

The Knight's Kiss

Falling for Prince Federico

To Kiss a King

BOWEN, NEBRASKA

The Bowen Bride

A ROYAL SCANDALS WEDDING

More Royal Scandals titles will be available soon. For updates, please visit nicoleburnham.com, where you can subscribe to Nicole's Newsletter.

Subscribers receive exclusive content, including the short story *A Royal Scandals Wedding*, an inside look at the wedding of Megan Hallberg and Prince Stefano Barrali from the novel Scandal With a Prince.

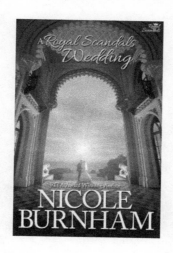

ABOUT THE AUTHOR

Nicole Burnham is the RITA award-winning author of over twenty novels, including the popular Royal Scandals series.

Nicole graduated from an American high school in Germany, then obtained a BA in political science from Colorado State University and a JD/MA from the University of Michigan. She lives near Boston, spends as much time as possible at Fenway Park, and travels abroad whenever she can score cheap airfare.

Readers may visit Nicole's website and subscribe to her newsletter at nicoleburnham.com.

facebook.com/NicoleBurnhamBooks
twitter.com/NicoleBurnham
instagram.com/nicole.burnham